SHADOWBOUND

KINGDOM QUEST 5

DR. BILL SENYARD

To my wife and editor, Eunice—thank you for your love, sharp edits, and endless support. This book is ours.
To my family—your encouragement means everything.
To my God, whose relentless love chases the unlovable, unloved, unlovely, unworthy, and unlikely (me included) without ever giving up—thank You for astonishing grace.
And to my grandkids, my biggest fans and story cheerleaders: Malcolm, Martin, Serena, and Remi—thank you for lighting up Paw Paw's world. (More grandkids, more tales ahead!)

NOTE TO READERS:

As always, no dragons, elves, or gnomes were physically harmed in the writing of this book. A few had their feelings hurt by the alleged negative representations. It turns out, dragons can be as sensitive as humans. Who knew? We regret any discomfort caused by the story.

Also, all dragons, gorgons, elves, magic man-bags, and giants appearing in this work are fictitious. Any resemblance to entities, living or dead, is purely coincidental.

One last thing. Unfortunately, a few readers of *Shadowbound* who, bless their hearts, have been tempted to draw parallels to the ancient and troubling Biblical book of Job. Although we acknowledge some similarities, unsubstantiated observations could be viewed, especially in certain legalistic circles, as a potential form of plagiarism— King forbid that anything like that could ever happen here. As you keen readers know, plagiarism involves taking someone else's language, ideas, or material without giving proper credit. In this age of AI, such practices are generally frowned upon by publishers, authors and prophets alike. Therefore, any resemblance to Job or other Biblical (or non-Biblical) works must be wildly coincidental.

Thank you for your understanding and patience as we navigate these literary complexities.

I

SHADOWBOUND

The great throne room was conspicuously silent, save for the restless flickering of torches casting jagged shadows on the marble walls. At the room's center, the Great King sat on his golden throne, his expression unreadable.

Shocking to everyone in the room, standing in front of the King was his greatest nemesis, Dolos, the vile Gorgon—a serial conniving schemer who had never missed an opportunity to embarrass or undermine the King, though, to be honest, he had failed in every attempt. Today, however, he exuded an inexplicable confidence that was deeply concerning.

Draped in the illusion of his alter ego, Sir Henry Dolos III, he cut the figure of nobility. Of course, no government had ever knighted him, nor had there ever been a Henry Dolos I, II or IV (thank the King for that). Yet to the uninformed, he radiated power.

Tall—easily over six feet—he carried himself with the unshakable poise of a man who had never been denied anything in his life. His sharp, aristocratic features were framed by neatly styled dark hair, silvered at the temples to lend an air of distinguished wisdom. His piercing blue eyes held the weight of a man accustomed to command.

Dressed in a bespoke three-piece suit, tailored to perfection, Dolos was the embodiment of old-world sophistication—at least on the outside. The deep charcoal fabric clung to his broad shoulders, and the crisp white shirt beneath provided a stark contrast against his tanned complexion. A navy silk tie, knotted with precise care, completed the look, while a gold signet ring on his right hand bore the crest of some unknown lineage—one he had surely fabricated.

His presence could dominate most rooms, but not this one. Here, he paled before the Great King.

Make no mistake: the King was hardly fooled by this entity standing before him. Dolos, the ancient gorgon, was no mere antagonist of legend—he was a dark manifestation of beauty corrupted and power twisted. When not in his disguise as a pretentious British royal, he was a vile serpentine. Once unveiled, his upper body retained a vaguely humanoid shape, sculpted with lean muscle like that of a warrior-angel fallen from grace. From the waist down, his body coiled into a massive, scaled tail that shimmered like oil on water, rippling with unnatural strength.

In his true form—his skin, if you could call it that, was the color of old marble, cracked with delicate veins of green and black. It pulsed faintly in dim light, as if something cursed slumbered beneath the surface. His face—once rumored to be striking—was half obscured by scales and shadows. His real eyes burned a hollow gold, slitted like a serpent's—unnerving and toxic. Oily, stringy red hair hung flat about his face. His bulbous eyes, wide and emotionless, shook with cold malevolent evil, their feral yellow tint strikingly lifeless.

Oh, it got worse. Dolos the gorgon was crowned with dozens of serpents writhing and whispering atop his vulgar, thin head. Each snake had its own glimmering eyes—some wide with hunger, others narrowed in anticipation of death. They moved as if tethered to Dolos' thoughts, quick to strike or coil in anticipation.

It is said by those who studied such things that Dolos was not born, but made—once a seer or prince, perhaps, cursed by a god or betrayed by kin. Whatever he was, whatever he became, only one thing is certain: he despises this King and would do whatever he could to tear him down.

In his present human form, he was mostly able to disguise his typical nauseating stench—some combination of vomit and thioacetone, which one chemist described as "worse than a decaying corpse dipped in sewage and left in the sun."

Still, Dolos's gaze was the opposite of the King's—cold, unblinking and merciless. They couldn't be more different.

In stark contrast, the Great King of Garden City reclined with ease upon his throne, radiating the quiet authority of a ruler who led not by fear but by presence alone. His robe— undeniably royal—was far from ceremonial. Its simplicity was deliberate, a subtle message: This official visit from Dolos did not warrant the effort of full regalia. He couldn't have been more dismissive if he were also flossing his teeth.

His robe flowed comfortably around him, pooling like soft shadows over the throne's polished arms. His feet were simply sandaled, his head left bare. Only his white hair and neatly shaped beard hinted at his royal status—groomed with care but not vanity.

Though his posture was relaxed—one leg crossed, fingers

absently tracing the carved lion that adorned the throne's armrest—his gaze was anything but. His eyes were steady, unblinking and clear, holding the kind of stillness that could silence even the most venomous of tongues. There was little doubt where the power rested in the throne room.

The tense silence lingered until the cold-blooded Dolos finally spoke. His voice was both erudite British and serpentine, the Queen's English slithering through the air with a discernible hiss.

"O Great King, please forgive my boldness, but none of your loyal aides"—he cast a quick, accusing glance at Nomos and Noomai—"will dare say it to your face. Your actual problem is not with me, nor with my followers. No, your majesty, the real embarrassment to your kingdom is humanity itself."

The room remained still and unresponsive, so Dolos pressed on.

"You have invested so much in them—time, energy, resources. Your very reputation is tied to their fate. And yet, what have they given you in return? Need I remind you of the Great Rebellion? A shameful event, truly best forgotten."

The King's voice was calm but edged with steel. "Lest we forget your role in it, you pit viper."

Dolos waved a hand dismissively, highlighting his impeccably manicured fingernails. "Hmm, debatable, I'm sure." His lips curled into a smirk. "But today, I come with a mutually beneficial solution. A remedy that will solidify your reputation as a just and wise ruler. It is time, O King, to cut your losses."

He paused as if to consider his next words very carefully. But everyone knew that his obscene pitch had been deliberately constructed, word for word, and rehearsed incessantly. He dared to look directly into the King's regal eyes and said with a flourish:

"Humanity is broken. Faithless. Incapable of true loyalty."

The King showed little reaction, barely sparing him a glance. "Is that so, dust crawler?"

Dolos's smile widened. "It is as clear as the stars above. If you had honored me—or any other species—with such favor, your kingdom would be in a much stronger position. Look at Amaratzim. Need I say more?"

Dolos took a measured step forward.

"You shower humans with gifts, and they kneel. You make their lives comfortable, and they praise your name. But loyalty that is bought is no loyalty at all—it is a mere transaction—a devil's bargain."

As he said the last words, his mouth curled into a subtle, sinister arc—not quite a grin, but close enough to make your skin crawl. The faint upturn at the corners suggested amusement, as if he already knew something you didn't. It was a smile without warmth, without soul—a predator's smile. Cold. Calculated. Patient. One expected a reptilian tongue to flick outward.

The King's expression continued to show no response, in fact, little interest at all. Nomos, the Royal Vizier, and Noomai, the Royal Counselor, had been summoned to witness this audience—not to protect the King (he needed no such thing), but because he seemed to know what was coming. It would trouble them beyond measure. The game, so to speak, was afoot.

Dolos's voice turned sharp, daring to push further. "Are you so high in your gilded palace, so far removed, that you cannot see? Behind your back, your people whisper and shake their heads, confused by your foolish devotion to these undeveloped creatures. They do not understand. You are alone in this, Your Majesty."

"What is it about humanity that you still cling to?" continued the gorgon, with an oily silkiness. "Name one who is truly faithful. Even one."

The con was nearly complete. Now, the hook must be set.

Dolos's voice dropped, almost reverent. "I would wager that if you withdrew your favor—if you stripped away the comforts they take for granted—they would abandon you in an instant. They are no better than beasts driven by animal hunger and thirst alone. As long as you fill their plates, they will call you King. But take that away, and they will curse you. You have become a laughingstock, Your Majesty."

The King still sat unmoved. His bored gaze drifted to the great, ornate window of his palace, where the city stretched beyond—the people, the homes, the lives he had nurtured and protected.

A long silence.

The legendary Royal Vizier Nomos's stubby fingers instinctively tightened around his grand sword hilt. For as long as anyone could remember, it had been his responsibility to train the elite of elite knights and warriors of Garden City, with an eye to an eventual conflict with the very entity that now stood before the King. He had personally fought Dolos on numerous occasions. There was no love lost between them. He stood ready to fight once more.

The aged-but-ever-young Nomos was a short, burly gnome with an unruly shock of very white hair and a long, equally unkempt white beard. He was a bit on the portly side. His boyish blue eyes lit up when he cracked a joke. Nomos was not a person to be trifled with. Not at all.

I would be remiss not to tell you this about Nomos: He

was very Scottish, if you know what I mean. He usually wore a thick cotton shift. With each step, his stiff leather sandals would loudly snap, foreshadowing his presence. On more formal occasions, he would wear a very colorful tartan kilt. Kilts are a type of skirt for men, and he often donned a red cap. Nomos preferred calling it a Kilmarnock bonnet. In some circumstances, Nomos might say about Dolos, "He's all fur coat an' nae knickers," meaning he talks a big talk but can't back it up. Or "If ah had a face like his, I'd teach ma backside tae speak." You get the idea.

Today, Nomos was fully prepared for battle, clad in his complete fighting armor. Forged deep in the cavernous forges beneath the Elder Roots, its plates shimmered with an oil-slick gleam, not metal, not leather, but something ancient and alchemically enhanced.

Intricate etchings covered every surface—runes in looping gnomish script and angular dwarven glyphs, a blend of magic and machine. His chest piece was tightly fitted, reinforced at the ribs with overlapping scales that moved silently, like whispered secrets.

A high collar flared up behind his neck like a mechanical cowl. His boots, though fully armored, were padded with spell-woven felt—he could cross a marble floor without a sound. And at the center of it all, over his heart, was a small insignia etched in silver: the symbol of Nomos' clan, half-forgotten by most but never by him.

Nomos' grand sword was made of the best steel in the land —a weapon so oversized for his small frame that most mistook it for ceremonial. But once drawn, it told a different story.

Its edges were notched with marks of real battle. The hilt was wrapped in deep green wyrmhide, supple yet grippy. A faint hum pulsed from the weapon, like a forge still smoldering in its heart.

They called it Verdict—not because it delivered justice, but because once Nomos drew it, the argument was over. To underestimate Nomos because of his size was a mistake. To ignore the armor? A fatal one.

"Wi' all due respect," Nomos leaned in to whisper in the King's ear, "how's about ye let me lop this bog beast's heid clean aff his stinkin' shoulders, once an' for aw?"

The King did not respond but gave him a knowing look— a silent command to hold.

Elder Royal Counselor Noomai was also deeply concerned, yet her face betrayed nothing.

Though her health had recently begun to fail, she still stood tall, unyielding—like a mountain touched by weather but unmoved by storm.

Then, at last, the King spoke, his words shocking both Noomai and Nomos.

"Gorgon, would you include my faithful servant Reggie, the orphan magician, in that charge?"

Dolos barely concealed his glee. The bait had been taken.

The King continued: "I have known no one more faithful than him. He walks the walk. He serves me with a devotion you cannot begin to fathom. He loves me with the kind of loyalty only humanity can offer. Once again, you have always disappointed me, Dolos. But Reggie? Ah… He has never wavered. He would follow me honorably no matter what."

Dolos nearly trembled with excitement. "That street rat? Oh, Your Majesty, impressive devotion—for a human. I'll give you that. But look at how you have blessed him! You knighted him, after all. That is no test of loyalty. Anyone would 'love' you if you gave them knighthood, oh yes, and had an award-winning story written about them."

Dolos sneered. "Here's a thought. A gentleman's wager, shall we? Let's put him to the test. Strip it all away—his wealth, his comfort, his friends, his reputation. And we shall see what is truly in his heart. Let's see if he still sings your praises when the world turns against him. Let's see if he remains faithful—or if he condemns you as a fraud."

Nomos stiffened. Even Noomai's unreadable mask faltered for a fraction of a second.

But the King? The King remained emotionless and silent. Dolos' face glistened with perspiration that carried the vile smell of a refuse swamp in late August.

Then, slowly, the King nodded. "You may have him."

Nomos gasped loud enough for all to hear. Dolos's grin split wide, but the King's voice cut through his triumph like a blade.

"But you may not kill him."

Dolos placed a hand over his chest in mock sincerity. "Of course, Your Highness." But silently to himself, he added forebodingly, "Ah, but there are far worse things than death."

"For this to be a true test, O King," the despicable gorgon rattled on, "the boy must not be made aware of our bargain. Anyone can rise above a trial if they know its end and purpose. No one can tell him his faithfulness is being measured. No one…" he glanced despisingly at Noomai and Nomos, "can intervene to spare the boy any aspect of the wager. Are we agreed?"

Nomos made another loud, gruff grunt.

"And when he proves successful?" inquired the King with eyes raised.

"Yes, you mean *if*, I am sure. If Reggie endures, oh, let's say, seven levels of trials without officially cursing you, then I would be proven wrong, of course. Ah, but if he fails—of which I have little doubt—you will be forced to admit that humanity's flaw is irredeemable."

A long pause.

The King's gaze darkened as he nodded his acceptance of the rules. "Begone, vile worm. But know this—you underestimate my servant. You underestimate humanity."

Dolos only laughed—a slow, slithering sound of delight.

The game had begun. The trap was set.

But what trap?

2

THE STORYTELLER

Alright, it's time to introduce myself. I'm Jeremy, the Senior Storyteller for the King. I've been rocking this gig for what feels like forever—ten years, but who's counting, no cap? Sorry if this breaks from the usual storytelling rules and style. This is me—the real me—before the Royal Editor gets hold of the text. No judgment. She does a great job making me sound like I have zero Gen Z accent at all.

Why this unusual reveal now? Because this time, I'm not just chilling on the sidelines—I'm in the thick of it, and it's lit! Normally, I hang out in the castle, digging up the juiciest details on the King's quests through research and interviews. Then my squad and I turn them into epic tales that are straight fire and super gripping.

Sometimes, though, I jump in way deeper. If you've read *The Garden Tale*, that was me all the way. I wasn't just writing it—I was out there, part of the elite crew that saved a whole version of Garden City from being wrecked by that sus gorgon, Dolos.

It's happening again, kinda. This time, my ride-or-die, the legendary Royal Vizier Nomos himself, pulled me into the quest with a personal invite.

Right after that shady meeting with Dolos, Noomai and a totally frustrated Nomos bounced to Noomai's low-key office in the castle. They sent a messenger to grab me ASAP. When I rolled in, the room was dead quiet, thick with worry and vibes I couldn't quite clock. I'd never seen either of them this stressed.

"Storyteller," Nomos said without even looking up. "I'm no' doin' ye any favors here. I need ye tae record this wild quest an' make sure it gets archived in the sacred records—the ones guarded by the Drukyl dragons."

"Of course, my crew. I'm here to help however I can—for you and the King, no cap."

Noomai didn't even glance my way. Something was up, for sure.

Noomai was the King's Royal Counselor Emeritus, a dope role she'd held for as long as anyone can remember. Some say she's like the heart of the King—and he'd vibe with that 100%. Back in her younger days, Noomai rolled with people on quests, dropping wisdom and good energy. She'd always say, "In other kingdoms, quests are how you earn the king's favor. Not here. No matter what goes down, this King will never think less of the ones he sends out."

She would remind them: "The King's favor is not based upon the success of your quest. The quest is a manifestation of that favor so that honor, glory and name might be experienced by those he *already* favors. This King is not what he appears, and his quests are equally inscrutable."

Though Noomai no longer joined questers, her righteous presence was still felt deeply in the Kingdom. Her eighty-plus years had certainly taken their toll—her body, now frail, was supported by a modest wooden cane—but nothing had diminished the joy in her chocolate-brown face or the light in her deep azure-blue eyes. Noomai was still a force to be reckoned with. This is a fact. Dolos feared and hated no one more than Noomai—except for maybe the King.

Today, she sat across a modest table from Nomos, blowing gently on a steaming cup of her favorite beverage—Taylor's of Harrogate Yorkshire Tea. She rarely went anywhere without it. With a smile, she would proudly say to anyone who shared a cup with her, "I've heard it's not for everyone. It's rich and slightly bitter, yes, but its aroma fills the room with a sense of welcome, of home."

And it really did.

The warrior-gnome, Nomos, presented a stark contrast to Noomai. While she exuded wisdom and grace, Nomos embodied strength and spirit in a way only a seasoned warrior could. The King trusted him above all others. Nomos was no random fighter; he was the Royal Vizier, having trained and mentored almost every great warrior in the Kingdom. Don't mistake his short, rounded stature, bright blue eyes and bushy white eyebrows for just another grandpa. My homie is not to be messed with.

Yo, check it. You should know, if you don't already, that Nomos is very Scottish—a fact that only added to his indomitable presence and the rich stories he shared about his homeland.

Noomai and Nomos filled me in with everything they could recall from what happened minutes before—the sketchy meeting with Dolos. The King was putting Reggie in danger? How could that be? I just shook my head.

"Ah, my old friend, what's going through that bushy head

of yours?" said Noomai graciously to Nomos, breaking the awkward, heavy silence.

"Aye, I dinnae mind sayin', I'm totally wiped!" Nomos replied, shaking his head. "I've got a knot in ma belly that winnae quit. I cannae wrap ma mind around what just happened. Wi' all respect tae ma King, I'm startin' tae wonder if his bum's oot the windae. I love him and would follow him anywhere, anytime. There've been plenty o' times he's given me orders I didnae get. But I've never been more troubled than noo."

Nomos leaned forward, both of his round elbows firmly planted on the table, and rubbed his square, bearded face—obviously concerned. "Reggie's still healin' from his parents' wrongful death, which he first blamed the King for. Wasnae he the one who saved the whole continent o' Amaratzim from chaos and war? Doesnae he deserve a break for that? Nay, instead, this wild, reckless bet that'll just hurt the poor laddie more. Is that fair? Is that right? Nay, it's neither kind nor okay. I trust the King wi' everything I've got, but this is tough."

"I know," said Noomai. "Of course, all of that is true—every word of it. We must ask ourselves: When was the last time the King ever let Dolos pull the wool over his far-reaching eyes? When has that reptilian dimwit ever come close to achieving his objective of shaming the King or anyone in the King's service? And when has the King ever unjustly mistreated those who have proclaimed their loyalty to him as their King? And so, in this case, while on the surface things seem unjust, it cannot be so."

Nomos threw his hands up. "So, what then? What could the King be thinkin'? Sendin' a laddie intae that monster's grip—alone."

"Dear Nomos," said Noomai, "we both know this is no

ordinary boy. Yes, he's just 19, but he's been through so much. Inside, he's a fully grown man, and he's already bested Dolos once."

"Aye, ma lady," Nomos grumbled. "But that was wi' help from a mighty Troll king swingin' a club the size o' Garden City! This time, he'll be solo—no clues, nae backup. It's too much. I get the King's love for quests, sure, and he can call them whenever—but this... this is straight-up gyte (crazy). Tell me I'm wrong. Storyteller, ye're ma witness. I dinnae like this one bit."

"Oh, dear me," said Noomai, looking directly into Nomos' troubled eyes. "I can see you've taken a liking to the magician. So have I. And so has the King. He holds young Reggie in the same esteem he once held Prince Yeled—and even his own son, Sarshalom."

[Storyteller's Note: You can read about Sarshalom and his incredible sacrifice in the Tale of the Unlikely Prince. *It's an epic read.]*

"And keep in mind, my friend, the King never uses quests to *prove* worth—that thinking is Dolos' alone. Rather, the King so be's quests so the already favored and worthy quester may experience more glory and name."

"Aye, that's true! But this feels different," Nomos shot back respectfully. "The King's steppin' back, leavin' Reggie exposed and vulnerable. This quest... Reggie cannae turn tae the King for help. He cannae expect rescue. We cannae step in either. He can cry oot for answers, but none will come. This isn't like any quest I've seen. I wouldnae blame the laddie if he did curse the King."

"Hear me noo. This quest will break him, Storyteller," Nomos said to me seriously, his voice full of worry. "If he survives, he'll be shattered—so broken that Noomai herself will spend the rest o' her days tryin' tae rebuild his sense o' self."

Even Nomos—tough, unbreakable Nomos—was shaken.

"Nomos, I've never heard you speak like this," I said, setting my quill down and adjusting my spectacles with a furrowed brow. "What is going on? Tell me everything. I serve the King, and so I serve Reggie as well, totally. Fer real."

Nomos paused, took a slow breath, then reached into his embroidered vest, retrieving his most prized possession—a long, elegantly curved Scottish pipe.

The craftsmanship was excellent. The deep brown grain caught the candlelight just so, revealing intricate whorls in the wood. The curve of the stem spoke of Edinburgh's finest artisans—a relic of a home long left behind.

He carefully placed the pipe between his lips—not to smoke, for he had given up that habit decades ago, but simply to *wear* it, as he liked to say. The pipe was as much a part of him as the spectacles perched on his nose.

"There's naught like it," he murmured, runnin' his fingers along the stem, glad for a quick distraction. "Look at this grain—see how it catches the light... and that smooth finish. I've been offered a fortune for it, ye ken." He turned it, watching the fire's glow dance on it. "But nay, I couldnae part wi' it. Some things are worth more than gold."

He set it down and gathered his thoughts.

I took a moment to toss some Bazooka Bubble Gum into

my mouth. I don't smoke, but I can, like, blow some humongous, sick bubbles. It helps calm my nerves and adds to my focus. And I am not ashamed to admit it—I geek out on Bazooka Joe and Mort. I read the cartoon in my pack. Mort says, "I got these medals at school." Joe asks, "What did you get them for, Mort?" Mort replies, "One I got for good memory... and the other one... I don't remember." Now that's the bomb comedy, true dat? If you don't think that's funny, you're just a poser. No judgment.

But anyway—back to the story.

Nomos finally spoke again. "The real horror o' it is this—this whole cursed quest was designed by Dolos himself."

I nearly dropped my quill. "What? That's wild."

"Aye."

"The King allowed this?" I asked.

"He did more than allow it," Nomos sighed, his eyes shadowed with something heavy. "A vile wager was made. The terms were set. An' if the King had been willin' tae touch the beast, they'd have shaken hands on it."

A chill hit me. "That's crazy. What in the King's name is he thinkin'?"

Nomos exhaled. "Aye, that's the question, is it no'?"

More silence stretched between us. Noomai graciously chose to sip her tea and let Nomos ponder the situation for a time.

"My dear friends, I'm worried for the boy too," Noomai finally responded quietly, thinking this was the time to speak on behalf of the Great King. "I imagine Reggie will believe he's being punished for something. We humans tend to assume that by default. But we both know—he's done nothing wrong. Even the King has praised his faithfulness more than once."

"I will say this. Dolos is right. Humanity does seem to carry a flaw. I once heard a scholar call it the *Retribution Principle*. It's hardwired into how we view the world and ourselves: if we do wrong, we expect punishment. If we do right, we believe we deserve reward."

"But Reggie?" I said, "he's been nothing but faithful. Loyal to the King in every way. So, what happens in his mind when he's forced to endure what will feel like punishment—without cause? How will he even begin to make sense of it?"

"Och aye, it's a foul tangle in the heid, sure enough," muttered Nomos, sharp as a thistle. "And dinnae think he'll get answers from the King. His Majesty must hold his tongue. Even that silence will feel like another lash to his soul."

"Yes, it certainly seems that way," agreed Noomai with a sigh. "But I think we are asking the wrong question here. Did you notice, like I did, that while Dolos appeared to be manipulating the King, forcing him into a deal he didn't want, it seemed to me that the King's hand was all over this—as if he was the one who crafted this wicked bargain, drawing Dolos into it unknowingly?"

"Wait, are ye sayin' the King designed this quest?" Nomos asked, eyes wide in shock. "The King put Reggie in this mess because he wanted tae, nae because he had tae?"

"Yes, that's my belief," confirmed the Royal Counselor. "The King wasn't blindsided or even shocked by Dolos' proposal. He invited us to witness it. I'm certain he knew exactly what was going on. I'm not suggesting he suspected Dolos' scheming—no, this was the King's plan from the very beginning. It's Dolos who doesn't realize he's already lost, that he's a mere pawn in the King's game."

"Hmmm," Nomos allowed himself a slight grin at last. "You think the King is letting Dolos think it was his own grand idea—that he spun the web himself. A sneaky wee trap... spidery, subtle, an' nae a chance of slippin' out. Aye, that would be just like this King."

Nomos paused for a moment to ponder the concept as a whole. His pipe moved slowly up and down between his lips as if it helped him concentrate.

"But are ye sayin' then that the King so be's evil and the unjust?" Nomos asked, his brow furrowing once more.

"Of course," answered Noomai with great confidence. "If by that you mean the King freely uses both good and evil to construct his so be'd quests? You and I both know the King is not what he seems. He ordains every quest in his Kingdom— the good and the bad, the evil and the righteous. There's no contradiction here. Every quest, even the darkest and most despairing, serves a greater purpose, well beyond our comprehension, mind you. When we're on a quest, especially when we're at the mercy of the enemy or drowning in failure, we don't see the purpose—we can't. We might even come to doubt the King's goodness and faithfulness. That is only normal. But nothing could be further from the truth. It's comforting, though, to know, notwithstanding what we see or feel in the moment, there is a higher power behind it all—the good King's design, woven through both the heroes and villains, the victories and defeats, the just and unjust, the good and evil, the honor and shame."

"If yer right... and I'm no' saying ye are—what's the point o' this doo-lally (craziness) then?" Nomos blurted out, running a hand through his graying red beard, still unsettled by the disagreeable audience with Dolos.

"Now, *that's* the real question, my friends," said Noomai, shaking her head. "There's something else at work here, something I can't quite grasp. All I can say is Reggie was meant to be on this quest, at this time, facing Dolos alone—all in the service of the great King. And that's the part that gives me hope.

"Despite everything—how unjust, how unfair it is on the surface, the presence of evil and good—I believe that in the end, we'll witness a victorious quest, more momentous than any we've seen before."

"If Dolos is merely a pawn in the King's plan, that is indeed very comforting—and even barry (good)," Nomos remarked, raising an eyebrow.

"Yes," Noomai replied. "All I know is that the King's plan will unfold, and nothing—not even Dolos—can stop it. In the end, even Reggie will agree... in the end." Her voice tailed off as she contemplated her premise even further. She blew gently on her steaming tea, causing the nutty, earthy aroma of the Harrogate to fill the room.

"I have seen it with other quests," Nomos said thoughtfully. "I think o' Yeled, or Anelé, or so many others. But theirs were different. They could've turned down their quests. But Reggie cannae. This is different. He doesnae even know what's happenin'. He'll have tae guess why the King seemingly abandoned him tae the whims o' Dolos. He might even curse the King. Then what?"

"Yes, I am troubled about that as well," she went on. "We can't always see the end from where we stand. In dark moments, we can't seem to wrap our weary fingers around shadowy high providence. It'll feel like everything depends on us and our choices, or on chance, skill, fate or fortune. Our minds can become filled with despair, doubt or fear, and we will automatically turn to blaming ourselves or others. The King has no such limitations. His ways are far higher than ours. For now, we must accept that so much remains unanswered. It's troubling, I know. It appears the King has disregarded Reggie's free will... and yet, we cannot fathom the greater plan at play. Perhaps the King is guiding him to something far greater than Reggie could ever imagine or would ever choose on his own."

"My dear lady, ma heid's yet mince! Is the King nae bound by Reggie's permission?" Nomos asked, still confused.

"No," Noomai responded, then paused to make sure she chose the right words. "Remember, our King is not what he appears. This King sees what Reggie cannot. He alone can see what lies ahead—where the myriads of paths begin and end. If it were required that the questers have full knowledge of all quests before they accede to the King's invitation, what would be the point of questing? No doubt, the King has established a grand end for the lad. It must be so. He has never failed to do right in the end. All evil and good alike—pains, losses, failures and successes—are all skillfully woven together along with Reggie's desires, needs and choices to complete the tapestry of glory and name the King has divined for Reggie, unaware and without permission. The King's design is never arbitrary."

"So, what do we, like, do now?" I asked, already knowing the answer.

"We trust the King," Noomai replied. "That is *our* little quest, I believe. In the end, the good will outweigh the bad. We cannot see the end at the beginning, but we can trust that the King does. Perhaps that's for the best. There is a purpose behind every quest, even those that seem unfair or overwhelmingly difficult. This Kingdom is ordered by a providence that stretches far beyond our vision or creativity. The King's ways—his plan—are far beyond what we can see.

It's difficult to accept, but we must trust that all things, good or bad, work together for the ultimate good."

"Reggie's task will be unbearable, if I know Dolos," Noomai continued thoughtfully. "We know Dolos particularly despises Reggie after what he did to him not that long ago."

[Storyteller's Note: You can experience the epic battle in "The Tale of the Orphan Magician."]

"Knowing Dolos," she continued, "the seven levels of his vile game will be designed to hurt the lad to his core. I don't imagine anyone in their right mind would ever have chosen this battle—or even agreed to it—if they knew. That's the nature of serving this King. It is also the nature of his quests."

"So, is the King gonna save the day, then?" Nomos asked, rubbing his long, unkempt beard.

"Perhaps," Noomai replied. "It depends on what you mean by that. But it appears this particular bargain is designed so that the King cannot come to Reggie's aid. That's above my understanding. All I know is Reggie is not separated from the King. We know that is not possible. Also, there is no power, no scheme and no lie that has the slightest dominion over this King. I suspect the King has something up his royal sleeve, and we'll be there to assist when the time comes."

"Please trust me here," assured Noomai. "It is not Dolos using the King—it is the opposite. Our King is playing Dolos and this devil's bargain like a skilled fisherman plays his catch, to give young Reggie a very rare honor—an honor only given to the very few who have the loyalty and maturity to do the impossible. If I am right, Reggie has been chosen to crush the gorgon's head a second time. This defeat will bring even more shame to the vile overgrown amphibian—and more glory to Reggie. Can you imagine the songs and books that will be written about the orphaned teenager who crushed the gorgon's skull twice?"

"Then yer sayin' the ends justify the means?" Nomos asked, though he knew the answer—not that he liked the answer much.

"Aye, on the King's so be'd quests, I do believe that it is so. I find great comfort in that, my warrior friend," said Noomai. "Can I make you some tea?"

"Nae, I'm afraid your Harrogate tea is not strong enough for what I need."

"But why Reggie?" That was the question clawing at me. "Why him?" I clenched my jaw. "So, like, what's Dolos' endgame? Revenge? That's so... so out there."

"Maybe pure, unadulterated revenge." Nomos rubbed his temple. "Last time they met, Reggie left Dolos wi' a burnt face an' a crushed skull. Dolos does nae forget such things. He'll make him suffer—an' he'll make it public."

"I wonder," Noomai began, "if Dolos chose Reggie not for revenge but because of his loyalty to the King. The King himself has said it—twice—no one is more faithful. And if Dolos can turn him, if he can make Reggie take the King to trial..."

Noomai let the words hang in the air.

"Then no one is safe," I finished, my voice barely above a whisper. "That's so wack," I said, shaking my head.

Nomos nodded gravely. "Aye, it's pure wack, so it is. If young Reggie goes down... what hope's left for the rest o' us?"

A deep, sus feeling settled in my gut.

"So, the King agreed to this because he, like, thinks Reggie won't break?" I asked.

"Aye," agreed Nomos. "The lad is tough, fer a human that is."

"But Reggie is wounded," I argued. "My guy has deep relational scars and unresolved grief. That makes him vulnerable."

Nomos gave me a hard look. "I know. That's what I tol' Noomai."

"That's straight fire! What can we do?"

"For now, Storyteller, we watch," Noomai said, leaning forward, voice low and firm.

"I will say this, though, an' it brings me some measure o' comfort," said Nomos. "Noomai believes that because o' the overwhelming risks an' near impossibility o' success—at least by human standards—this quest must lead tae the greatest o' all honors, the highest attribution o' glory an' name. An' on the flip side o' the coin, this would be Dolos' most painful an' humiliatin' defeat at the hands o' anyone other than the King himself. A mere human lad shaming the chief slippery squid twice."

"Otherwise... how could any of this make sense?" I nodded sadly.

"But we don't just sit by," Nomos continued, his voice taking on an edge. "We watch closely. We make sure Dolos plays by the rules."

"And if he doesn't?"

Nomos let out a long breath, his fingers curling more tightly around the stem of his pipe.

"Then we step in," he said forebodingly.

～

As I sit here, the ink drying on the page, I can't shake the unease gnawing at my chest.

I know what some of y'all are thinking.

"But what if Dolos is the good guy? What if the King is the manipulative one? Or maybe he is losing it? What if we've been wrong this whole time?"

Yeah. As if. King forbid.

Lemme be clear to the max: Dolos is a world-class deceiver. Dude could convince you the sky is yellow, that taxes are optional, or that he's a misunderstood anti-hero fighting the system. He's a shapeshifter, and not in the 'cool mythical creature' way—he shifts perception. He is gaslighting incarnate. One day, he's a posh British lord charming his way through high society. Next, he's a rogue scholar dropping wisdom like he'd written the ancient texts himself. And the worst? Sometimes, he plays the underdog, the tragic revolutionary sticking it to the so-called oppressors.

And you know what? He's totally good at it.

Plenty of smart people—way smarter than me—have totally fallen for his act. Don't believe me? Read *Tale of the Unlikely Prince*. Dolos basically adopted Prince Yeled, turned him into his own personal puppet, until Noomai came through and, like, shut that all the way down. And guess what? Yeled wasn't much older than Reggie.

Which... brings us to this absolute mess of a story.

Now, look, I've tried to stay neutral here. I have. But I gotta be real. Dolos? Couldn't trust him as far as you could yeet a full-grown Precairan Troll (which, by the way, *don't*— they're rabid, always, and extra cranky after eating, say, fifty lambs and a dozen giraffes). You get the picture.

But let's, like, put Dolos on the shelf for now.

Let's talk about Reggie—a kid I actually care about—a

friend I would move literal mountains for if it meant keeping him safe. But guess what? I can't. I've been explicitly told that no matter what happens, I am not allowed to step in. Harsh.

Why?

Because a quest has been, like, ordained.

Usually, that's fantastic news. When the King sends you on a quest, you're set. By the end, you get the full hero treatment—knighthood, songs in your honor, maybe even a fancy title with "Lord" or "Duke" in it.

But this time? I'm with Nomos. This time, the quest feels insane—totally wrong.

And literally—I've never been so blindsided in my entire life. Like, I felt actual shockwaves reverberate through my skull.

How could this be happening?

What does it mean for Reggie? For the King? For the entire Kingdom?

And honestly? What does it mean... for me?

The King has committed to never intervening. No matter how much Reggie cries out, no matter how much he pleads for answers, for guidance, for anything—there will be only silence. I fear that silence may break him. I fear it may break us all. Truth.

Thanks for your patience during this personal, unedited and naked interlude. It is time for me to get back to my job as a professional storyteller and have all my charming slang edited clean, totally.

3

THE SHADOWBOUND QUEST

The first thing Reggie felt was biting cold—not the crisp waft of morning air, but something deeper, more insidious. It coiled around him like an unseen force, creeping into his bones, numbing his fingers, pressing against his chest like an invisible, frigid weight.

Only moments ago, he had been in his hometown, Buzah, dazzling the morning commuters with his sleight of hand under his stage name, Raziel the Magnificent. Ever since playing a crucial role in saving the city, he had become a local celebrity. People still told the tale of how he had outwitted an entire dwarven army, luring them into dragon territory, and how he had tricked a pirate armada into believing they were about to be ambushed by a massive fleet—only for them to realize, too late, that it was nothing more than a scattered formation of fishing boats.

Songs had been written about the orphan magician Reggie. A play was even set to open in Qayeen next year in his honor, not to mention an award-winning book for young readers called *The Tale of the Orphan Magician.*

Even the children adored him, begging for his autograph. He had woven that into his performances, making it a signature trick: "Is this your card?" he would ask, raising an eyebrow with a knowing smirk. And to the audience's amazement, they would find their selected card already signed with his name—a guaranteed crowd-pleaser. No one could manipulate cards better than this street magician. It was as if he were cosmically linked to them.

Felix, his talking magic pouch, a glowing—a sarcastic enchanted backpack that regularly talks in memes—often chimed in, rolling his imaginary eyes.

"A signed card? Can't you give them something useful, like a toothbrush or toilet paper? Your signature isn't even worth half a cup of coffee."

Their sharp, practiced repartee always led to laughter from the crowd—children and adults alike.

Though his history was still a bit of a mystery, Felix had been a gift from one of the great Magi of the Drukyl dragons, with whom Reggie had lived for a few years. The Drukyl dragons were renowned for their grasp of the magic arts. However, they were very careful not to use them outside their country at the northern mountainous extremes of Amaratzim. To them, Reggie—or Raziel the Magnificent—was family.

When Reggie left their care to return to his people in the country of Qayeen, the greatest spellcaster of Drukyl created a magic pouch from a single special thread, imbued with a quirky, odd personality and the name Felix. The wizard's hope was that this talented former orphan, Reggie, would never be alone. That was copacetic with Felix as well. Reggie and Felix had grown to be the closest of friends. I should mention that Felix, the magic pouch, has made it known he prefers to be called a man-bag. I shall do just that.

The audience always laughed at Felix's quips, well, most of them anyway. Life had been good for the two unlikely heroes of the recent war—a war that had nearly decimated the entire continent.

During the victory celebration a few months back, Reggie and Felix were honored by both the Great King of Garden City and the President of Qayeen. They not only received medals but, in an unprecedented move, had been knighted. It was the first time in history that a magic pouch—excuse me, a magic man-bag—had been granted knighthood by not one, but two national leaders. Felix had wrestled over his new title, torn between Sir Felix and Sir Man-Bag—fortunately, he had gone with Sir Felix.

For Sir Reggie, that moment was life-changing.

He had not always enjoyed such peace or honor in his life. He was orphaned as a child, his parents executed—accused of secretly supporting the Great King of Garden City. Qayeen was founded by rebels who had turned against the King generations ago, and even after all those years, the old wounds had never healed. The people of Qayeen still feared that one day, the Great King would send his armada to reclaim the land—even though that day never came.

As we all know, paranoia is a dangerous thing.

Whenever tensions flared, suspected King-lovers—mockingly called *kingies*—were rounded up, tortured and often executed. Among the tragic victims were Reggie's parents.

Can you imagine the psychological torment of an eight-year-old boy losing both his parents within days? Of course, there was nothing he could have done, but the mind is cruel that way. Deep inside, we all carry a dark, relentless dragon-voice skilled at weaving tight tapestries of guilt and shame.

Perhaps you, too, have heard its whispers: *"Why didn't I do more? Was it my fault? Why did I survive when they didn't?"*

As the days turned into months, and months into years, Reggie's sorrow festered into something darker. His bitterness grew, spreading like poison, until it was no longer only himself he blamed—it was everyone. The entire city of Buzah, every silent bystander, every coward who had looked the other way.

But no one—no one—was more despised in Reggie's heart than the Great King himself.

Where had the King been when his parents were slaughtered? Why had he done nothing? What kind of ruler allowed innocent people to suffer and die in his name?

The questions burned in his mind, unanswered. And so, Reggie's hatred became his compass, leading him down a path he never could have imagined.

Reggie was rescued by the Drukyl dragons, who took him in as one of their own. In their mountain sanctuary, he learned the art of magic and deception. The Drukyls, whose very DNA carried magic, taught him to weave illusions, misdirect the eye and manipulate perception. Though he lacked their inherent magic, he learned to imitate it with skill and precision. He was particularly gifted at card tricks.

At 18, Reggie, who humbly took on the stage name Raziel the Magnificent, went back to his hometown of Buzah, primarily to be with humans again. With no family, no home, no source of any income—he was a shadow. It didn't take him long to see there were many teens like him, living on the streets, begging for coins and food, digging through the putrid dumpsters behind fast-food joints and bakeries.

He decided to make a difference and started the Street Shadows, an inner-city home for street rats and runaways

who, like him, had no other family. He and Felix found an
abandoned warehouse at the docks, and it became home for so
many unfortunate boys, girls, dragons, gnomes, elves and
even a sleepy giant named Fritz. The Street Shadows
expanded to multiple warehouses and provided a safe place to
live but also offered work and internships in the construction
of furniture, sails, boats and almost anything anyone might
want.

What did Reggie get out of it? Some healing, I suppose.
Perhaps it made him aware there was some good in the world
—that there were people and other species who you *could*
trust to have your back when things go downhill. But most of
all, it gave him a sense of family again.

When Reggie turned 19, the Great Buzite War erupted.
The vile gorgon Dolos conspired with the dwarven nation of
Shelamot and the King of Oyevski to invade Qayeen. Their
plan was brilliant. Their forces were overwhelming.

They should have won.

But Reggie and Felix, aided by the Eagle Secret Service
(ESS)—the elite special forces of the Great King—
surprisingly intervened. The ESS was an extraordinary unit,
composed of warriors from all species, trained not only in
knightly combat but also in crossbow sniping, sabotage,
explosives, humorous banter and unconventional warfare.

Together, they turned the tide, defeating the massive
armies of two countries, a pirate armada, and, of course, badly
shaming Dolos himself.

At the war's end, Reggie finally met the Great King face
to face. What he saw shook him to his core. The King's gaze
held something he never expected—his mother's eyes. For a
moment, he felt loved, honored. He had found the father love
he subconsciously longed for.

The rage that had consumed him for years began to crack. He saw the King not as an enemy but as someone worthy of loyalty.

From that day forward, he served the Great King not only as a subject but as a friend.

But now...

Everything was about to change. And not for the better. Reggie's entire world was going to be ripped away—with the approval of the King. Oh my!

Reggie opened his eyes.

Dark clouds churned in a sickly purple sky, casting an eerie glow over the ruined landscape. Jagged mountains loomed in the distance, and beyond them, the skeletal remains of a castle jutted out like broken teeth. The land felt wrong— lifeless, twisted... watching.

And then, to Reggie's utter astonishment, he saw it—a frog.

A medium-sized, nondescript amphibian sat on a moss-covered rock beside him, his slick, greenish-brown skin pulsing with a faint, unnatural glow. His golden eyes—far too intelligent for a simple creature—blinked once before he spoke. Most absurd was the beat-up, oily top hat that sat leaning on his protruding head.

"Braaaap!" The frog let out a comical sound. "Ah. You're awake. That saves me the trouble of slapping you."

Reggie scrambled back, his hands pressing into the damp ground. "What on earth?"

The frog hopped closer, moving with an eerie, almost creepy grace.

"No time for shock, Quester."

Reggie frowned. "Quester?"

The strange, behatted frog gave a slow, knowing nod. "You have been unenviably chosen for the Shadowbound Quest. The only way out is to win—which is hardly likely at all. I suppose the word 'chosen' is quite unfortunate. In normal use, it implies an honor. This is anything but that, boy."

Reggie swallowed hard. He ignored the frog's disdainful tone. "A quest? Who has the authority to kidnap me and force me to be… wherever this is?"

The patronizing frog let out a slow, guttural croak. "Crooaaak, the Shadow Lord, of course."

Reggie understood. *Dolos. It had to be Dolos.* His stomach twisted.

The frog—Jinx, as he introduced himself—gave a slow nod and continued with his deep, throaty voice. "As I was saying before I was so rudely interrupted, you have been *chosen* for the Shadowbound Quest." The frog did air quotes as he said "chosen" with his itty-bitty frog appendages. It seemed pretty comical to Reggie, but he chose wisely not to mention it.

"The only way out is to win—and as I said already, good luck with that," the aloof amphibian droned on.

Reggie swallowed hard. "He can't merely whisk me away to this place and…"

"Yes," Jinx said, cutting him off, puffing up slightly, as if preparing for a grand speech. "The Shadow Lord obviously *can* and *has* cast you into this world—or as we prefer, 'level.' This is his twisted creation, filled with the appropriate monsters, death traps and impossible trials designed to break you and make you suffer. To be clear, we do not expect you to succeed."

Reggie let out a nervous laugh. "Well, that's encouraging. Thanks for the great pep talk. Shadow Lord? You've got to be kidding me, right? Is that what that idiot Dolos calls himself now? Really? Better the *Hot Mess* or the *Wanna-be King—Sir Stupid*, maybe. How's his skull from that little soiree he and I had with a Troll's club?"

The last time the two met, Reggie used sleight of hand with cards to distract the gorgon while a massive troll king belted him once, caving in much of his head.

Jinx remained silent. Reggie half-expected a chuckle from Felix, his ever-present companion. Felix would never miss an opportunity to tease Dolos. But there was only the sound of his own breathing. Concerned, he looked down at his belt, and to his shock, there was no man-bag. Felix was gone. For the first time in a long while, he was truly alone. A shiver ran down his spine.

"Oh yes," said the far-too-serious frog, raising one of his thin eyebrows. "Your rude talking pouch is not available to you until you can pay 15 diamonds."

"What are you talking about?"

"I was going to get to the rules in a moment, but alas, very well. To win your quest, you have only two chances. First, you must survive seven trials—or levels. I assure you, they are quite impossible, and even then, they will increase in difficulty. They range from impossible in the lower levels to 'way beyond even the possibility of possible' in the higher ones. As I said, you are not expected to survive. Current Las Vegas odds are +500,000. To give you an idea, the Cleveland Browns' chance of winning the Super Bowl is +30,000."

"So, you're saying I have a chance?" quipped Reggie, channeling his inner *Dumb and Dumber*.

Jinx tried to nod his head but could only shake his entire slimy body back and forth in an awkward, silly motion.

The frog's expression darkened. "No, the Shadow Lord wants you to fail. He still remembers how you publicly embarrassed him in the Qayeen Royal Hall. He can't wait to see you hurt and crying out for mercy."

"What a thoughtful person. I've missed him, too," Reggie said, mimicking Felix's typical sarcastic voice. That is what he would have said if he were here. Reggie felt a pang of vulnerability and isolation without his best friend.

"You said there were two ways to win the quest?"

"Yes, it is so. Brraaaapp!" Jinx croaked vulgarly in frog as he licked his lips—if that is indeed what they were—and nodded his head to the ground in front of the rock on which he was squatting. There was a small card, about the size of a business or game card, similar to a *Get Out of Jail Free* card familiar to most gamers. On it was written, *Go to Trial.*

The talking anuran continued, "At any time within the seven levels—unless you perish, of course, then the card is null and void—you can demand a trial before the High Court of all the land and charge the Great King with abandonment, indifference, disloyalty, bad hair and questionable hygiene in general."

Jinx chuckled. It's hard to tell with frogs, as you can imagine. "I added the last ones, but it is not necessary, actually. If found guilty, the court will issue an official legal curse against the King, signed by both you, of course, and the judge. Subsequently, the so-called Great King will have to admit that the Shadow Lord has won. Let him feel the shame of such a defeat for once."

"Why in the King's name would I do such a stupid, unfaithful thing?" exclaimed Reggie.

The frog stood up on his back legs. Reggie had never seen anything like it before. This was a very strange being. It was obvious why he adjusted his stance. He seemed to rise like a barrister who was going to make a great case before a jury. Looking around, as if he were in front of a great audience, he began—clearly a memorized script, no doubt prepared by Dolos.

"It is only a matter of time before you open your pathetic eyes and see that the Great King has been using you for his purposes. That is what he does. He is a master at treating people well—like making them knights of the realm. Still, when difficulties arise, he worries about his own well-being and reputation. He is not the good King he appears to be. Dolos... uh... Shadow Lord has been trying to get people to see that for many generations now. You may find the Shadow Lord's methods distasteful, but his singular goal is to expose the selfishness of this King. All that being said, he wants you to be the one to take him to court. In fact, anytime you want out, hand the card to me, and—whoosh—you will be safe and sound in the warm courtroom. Easy peasy."

Reggie's breath caught. "Wait... the King will put an end to this silliness forthwith. He will break into this shadow place and help me, any time now. You'll see."

Jinx's throat swelled as it let out a slow croak. "Foolish boy, Braaaaap! You don't think you would be here unless the King had so be'd it, right? I wonder—but this is just me—I wonder if you've upset or disappointed the King?"

A destructive tiny seed had been planted in Reggie's brain by the erudite frog. It often takes so very little to mess things up. A small grain of sand in the right place can ruin a great war machine.

"But it is only a stray thought of a humble servant—worth dwelling on later, to be sure—but you will soon be too busy to worry about that."

Reggie scowled and shook his head, hoping that he would wake up from this nightmare. "That makes no sense. I have been the picture of faithfulness to my King. It can't be... Wait, what... How am I supposed to know what to do?"

"That is why I am here. Think of me as your game show host—an amphibious Simon Cowell, Lilly Singh or Carson Daly. I for one, would prefer to be back at my pond. It is summer now, and the fattest mosquitoes are swarming, moving quite slowly due to their engorged size. I am missing the good meals. Ahem, never mind. Here are the rules of the game. You are to suffer seven levels, boy," the frog said, "boy" simply and disdainfully. "I should add that no one has ever made it all the way through. But hey, eventually, someone might?... Or not."

Reggie exhaled sharply. "Great. So, I'm supposed to blindly enter this...this quest... on my own?"

The frog hopped onto Reggie's shoulder, its small weight grounding him. For a slimy little creature, he smelled like something bigger and yuckier. Reggie noticed that while one of his large eyes rested upon him, the other jerked around all over the place—Reggie supposed, on the lookout for food.

"You are not as quick on the uptake as some others who have been on this Shadowbound Quest before," said the frog dismissively. "It is a bit disappointing. I repeat, the Shadow Lord expects you to lose. This is just punishment for you, yes?"

Reggie's stomach twisted into a knot, and he was getting colder by the second.

"See on your wrist?" the frog pointed his body to his left wrist. There was a leather bracelet with five small diamonds resting in a line. It looked like the bracelet was designed to hold more.

"We are not indifferent to your pathetic, unreasonably low survival chances. Even the guilty have some rights, I suppose. We have bestowed upon you five diamonds to begin your trials. If you ever lose all your diamonds, your life is forfeit. But if, by chance, you do survive a level, you will be awarded 10 more diamonds and a new identity or role that matches the context of your new level. The diamonds can be used at any time to purchase weapons and armor, heal wounds, get hints on riddles, ask a question of an oracle or, perhaps—as I said— you may choose to waste 15 precious life-diamonds to reunite with the grotesque, rude pouch friend. I wonder if that's worth it at all. And of course, at any time, you can play the *Go to Trial* card. I recommend that action be taken sooner rather than later."

Reggie was distracted by a deep, guttural growl rumbling through the air, vibrating through the cracked ground beneath him. Somewhere in the distance, armored figures moved through the mist—knights, but Reggie couldn't be sure. Their eyes burned with violet light; their swords jagged with darkness. He couldn't see where they were headed as they were hidden in the shadows, running away from the two.

Jinx leapt from Reggie's shoulder. "No time for second thoughts, Quester. Welcome to Level One: The Battle of the Dead. Your avatar has no weapons. They would do you no good anyway. You only have your wits, as pitiful as they might be."

"Wait, what is my identity?" yelped Reggie.

"For this level, you are The Death Slayer. Let it begin! Crrrroooakkk!"

"Death Slayer?" thought the boy. "That can't be good."

The bizarre quest had begun before Reggie could ask another question. He was confused, of course, but his brain had signaled the release of cortisol—the fight, flight or freeze steroid. Reggie was ready to fight. But fight what?

And somewhere, unseen, the King could only watch in silence.

4

LEVEL ONE: THE BATTLE OF THE DEAD

The moment Reggie opened his eyes, the cold had become noticeably sharper, more real—biting, in fact. Gone were the strange frog, the rocks and the shadows. His breath curled in front of him like pale smoke, and a jagged, frozen cavern stretched endlessly in all directions. The walls were smooth ice, reflecting a warped, ghostly image of himself wherever he looked. A single iron door loomed at the far end, its surface coated in frost.

As the strange amphibian guide had said, his hands were indeed empty.

His deck of cards, his coins, his magic wand—even the small silver whistle he always wore around his neck—were gone. The whistle was a gift given by the Drukyl dragons that he could use at any time to call for their aid. Gone.

He also didn't have his warm wool coat. It was spring in Qayeen, so Reggie was dressed in a T-shirt, jeans and worn tennis shoes. A dragon league baseball cap adorned his head, keeping his unkempt, long hair more or less in check.

A cruel chuckle echoed through the chamber. Reggie spun around. There, standing atop an icy pillar, was Dolos himself. The gorgon's serpentine hair slithered lazily, his stone-gray skin glistening with frost. His eyes gleamed with mischief.

Gorgons are grotesque amalgamations of man and beast, though not necessarily in that order. They are creatures of nightmares—twisted, unnatural—and steeped in malice.

Among them, Dolos stood above all. Twice the size of even the largest man, his hulking frame was a study in distortion—muscles straining against his warped form, his body bent as if it had been broken and reforged numerous times into something monstrous. His bulbous, glistening yellow eyes radiated malevolence from a skull crowned with a writhing nest of serpents. Their pale mouths gaped wide, venomous fangs perpetually bared, hissing in a constant, eerie chorus.

A rancid, matted beard clung to his chest, its tangled strands glistening with filth and decay. Swarms of bloated flies circled him in a grotesque dance, drawn to the sickly-sweet stench of festering rot that clung to his flesh like a curse.

[Storyteller's Note: Gorgons have existed since the earliest days of the Garden in the middle of Garden City. No one is quite sure who first named them, but the word itself means "grim" or "dreadful"—an apt description. Make no mistake, gorgons are formidable creatures and no ally of the King. Perhaps you've heard of the Medusa in your ancient Greek literature classes? If you looked at her face, you would immediately be turned to stone. She was also a gorgon, in fact, Dolos' eldest daughter. Fortunately, she received her gift of petrification from her mother's side.]

A thick, muscular tail lashed the ground behind Dolos, jerking with restless energy. Coiled around his broad chest and powerful waist, two massive, hissing serpents squirmed—ill-tempered, ever watchful. His reptilian arms, sinewy and scaled, hung at his sides.

Long, saurian fingers, tipped with jaundiced, painfully curved nails, clutched an enormous clock. It appeared ancient, its surface marred, its hands moving with a deliberate, ominous *tick-tock, tick-tock*. Each mechanical clink echoed with unnatural, ominous weight. Dolos grinned—a wicked, serpentine smile, filled with fangs too numerous, too jagged and too cruel for anything once human.

"Poor, poor Reggie," Dolos cooed with little pretense of

sincerity or compassion. "You look like you've lost something. Your tools, your tricks—your precious magic—oh, and your cute man-bag. What was his name? Fonsie? Feedly Dee? How will the great orphan magician ever escape now?"

Reggie clenched his fists. "I don't need tricks to beat you, Shadow Loser."

Dolos' grin widened, showing rows of pointed, stained teeth. "Oh, but you do. This is your punishment, my dear boy —not mine. You are about to be caught in a war that is not yours. You will see what loyalty costs. We all will."

Dolos laughed rudely at his own joke.

He gestured toward the iron door. "The rules are simple: you have one minute to unlock that door. If you fail, the cold will claim you. If you cannot make it through the door, you will freeze, and the city will be overrun—killing every man, woman and child there."

"Tick-tock, tick-tock."

A sudden gust of wind howled through the cavern. The frost on the door thickened.

"Tick-tock, tick-tock."

Reggie's heart pounded. "And where's the key?"

Dolos flicked his wrist. From the icy ceiling above, a key dangled by a thin thread of frozen webbing—far out of reach.

"You'll have to figure that out yourself," Dolos said with a smirk. "Tick, tock."

The gorgon vanished in a flurry of ice, putrid odor and smoke.

The countdown had begun.

Reggie's mind raced. *Think. Think.* He had no rope, no staff, no magic props. But he had something better—his wits.

He took a slow breath, centering himself. Then he looked

at the reflections in the ice walls around him. Mirrors were liars. He had used them before in magic tricks, bending light and misdirecting crowds. And right now, he needed them to lie again.

"Tick-tock, tick-tock."

He studied the reflections. The key looked far away—but in one of the reflections, it seemed closer.

That was it. He lunged toward the reflection that showed the key within reach, thrusting his hand out— his fingers wrapped around the frigid piece of metal.

For a second, his brain refused to understand what had happened. He had touched a reflection—no, an illusion—but the key had been real.

Dolos' tricks cut both ways.

"Tick-tock, tick-tock."

Wasting no time, Reggie sprinted to the door, shoving the key into the lock. His numb fingers fumbled, the ice creeping closer. The frost spread up his legs, burning his skin.

"Click."

The door swung open, and Reggie threw himself forward as the thick, frozen door behind him snapped shut, sealing the underground cavern in solid ice.

In the distance, he could still hear Dolos' vile laughter. This was not over.

Reggie glanced up in time to realize he was inside a walled city.

The air was thick with tension. Dozens of armored soldiers rushed back and forth, their boots pounding against the stone as they scrambled to prepare for an attack. A war horn blared from a high parapet, its mournful wail slicing through the chaos, summoning every defender to their appointed places.

Women and children darted through the streets, vanishing into the dark mouth of a cavern beneath the city—a bunker maybe, a last refuge, perhaps. Their hurried movements left an aching tightness in Reggie's chest. They knew what was coming.

And so did he.

Dolos's words echoed in his mind.

"You will be caught in a war that is not yours, boy. You will see what loyalty costs."

Reggie's stomach twisted again.

The soldiers were clearly desperate and caught unprepared. Many were fumbling to quickly put on their armor, their fingers grasping at straps and buckles in their rush. Some barely looked old enough to stay out past 10 p.m. They were boys pretending to be men in a war they could not win.

He seized the nearest soldier—a man trying to buckle his chest plate with trembling hands, sweat cutting muddy trails down his face. "What's going on?"

The anxious man glanced at him, startled, then back at his armor. "Friend, I don't know who you are or how you got inside these walls, but your timing is... unfortunate." His voice was grim. "The siege is upon us. And if the Great King doesn't intervene, it is only a matter of time before we fall."

"Who's attacking?" Reggie asked, a deep unease curling in his gut.

The soldier paused, his face darkening. "See for yourself. Go up on the parapet."

Reggie didn't hesitate. He ran.

The moment he reached the high wall, his breath caught in his throat. A sea of undead soldiers stretched as far as the eye could see. They stood in perfect ranks, unmoving, swords drawn, shields raised. Skeletal hands gripped weapons crafted from dark metal, jagged and cruel. Their hollow eye sockets burned with a violet fire—the same eerie glow Reggie had glimpsed in the shadows in the ice cave. Thousands.

The entire army stood in an unnatural silence, locked in place, no doubt waiting for a single command to attack. The blood-red sky above bathed them in a sickly glow, as if the battlefield had already been soaked in carnage. A thick, peaty fog enveloped each in a dark, ethereal fashion. This was an unnatural army already all too familiar with death and dying.

Reggie swallowed hard and took a breath.

"This isn't a war. This is a massacre waiting to happen."

He turned back toward the city. The defenses were pitiful —the walls were old, the soldiers were young. There were barely 200 men, most of them young and ill-equipped. Their armor was a patchwork of rusted metal, their weapons dull or hastily reforged.

They wouldn't last the night. Hey, they wouldn't last an hour.

His mind raced. There had to be a way out—some trick, some misdirection—something. But for the first time in a long time, he had nothing.

No allies.

No plan.

No escape.

No Felix.

His fingers brushed against the trial card in his pocket. He remembered: "Go to Trial, and it will all be over." But certainly, this can't be happening, can it?

"Would the King leave me here? Would he leave all of them here to face certain destruction? Am I being punished? For what?"

Reggie shoved the thoughts aside. "Focus. "

He spun toward a nearby officer—a grizzled man shouting orders over the wailing horn. "Take me to your King!" Reggie demanded.

The sergeant barely glanced at him before barking back, "We serve the Great King of Garden City, but he is not here. We have sent messengers, but there is no more time. We only have a young officer in charge, Commander Armstrong—not much older than you. But he was never prepared for this."

The words hit Reggie like a punch to the gut. "We are in the Great King's land. And he is not here? He has abandoned these people—his own people. It can't be so."

Reggie's pulse quickened even more. He tried to push the thought away, but it refused to leave. These men weren't traitors or rebels like the people of Qayeen had been. They were the King's own subjects. And yet—he was not coming for them.

Something about that sent a noticeable shiver down Reggie's spine. He had a sinking feeling that no one was coming to save him. This was his quest now. He couldn't expect the King's help—not this time. "What is going on?"

Reggie was led through the hastily assembled war camp, past soldiers rushing to fortify weak points along the walls. Fear was thick in the air, but they still fought to keep their hands steady as they prepared for the inevitable slaughter.

At the center of the command tent stood Commander Armstrong.

He was young—mid-20s at most—and far too well groomed for a man about to die. His uniform was crisp, his mustache and lambchop sideburns meticulously trimmed, his dark hair combed back without a strand out of place. But nothing could disguise the terror in his eyes.

He looked up as the sergeant entered. "Commander?"

"Yes, Sergeant Miller?" Armstrong's voice was calm, but a slight tremor was evident beneath it.

"You have a visitor. He claims he can help."

Reggie stepped forward, and Armstrong's eyes flickered with confusion. A boy. A street kid in casual clothes, wearing a baseball cap. "And you are…?" Armstrong asked, his brow furrowing.

Reggie straightened his shoulders. "My name is Reggie. I am an envoy of the Great King, sent to assist you."

It was a lie. Or was it?

The commander's expression darkened. "So, that means… the King is not sending an army?"

Reggie's heart sank. He hadn't meant to deliver that message—but maybe he did.

Reggie hesitated. "I... I can't say for sure. But we must assume that whatever forces he sends may be too late to do any good."

Armstrong let out a slow breath and ran a hand through his perfect hair. Not a single strand moved out of place. "Then we are alone."

That was becoming a recurring theme for Reggie.

"Give me a sitrep (situation report)," Reggie said quickly, trying to sound more confident than he felt.

Armstrong exhaled and leaned forward. "Defenses against an army of the dead? I wouldn't even know where to begin measuring that. Do you?"

Reggie shook his head. "I'll take my best guess. How many soldiers do you have?"

"A little over 100. Half of them have seen combat before. The rest? Untrained. Unprepared."

Reggie's stomach twisted a third time in a matter of minutes. "And the enemy?"

Armstrong's lips pressed into a thin line. "Scouts estimate 1,000 or more. All armed. All dead."

Reggie took a slow breath. "Are weapons effective against them?"

Armstrong gave a dry laugh. "That's the million-gold question, isn't it? I was hoping you could tell me."

Reggie bit his lip. He had nothing. No intel. No strategy. No idea what would work. But giving up wasn't an option.

He forced himself to focus. "What about the women and children? Where are they going?"

Armstrong nodded toward the cavern entrance in the city square. "There's a cave beneath the city, large enough to hold all of them. Water, food—enough to last a week. The tunnels stretch in every direction. Even if we fall, they should be safe until the King's forces arrive."

Something clicked in Reggie's mind. Tunnels. Would that work again? In the Great War, he had tricked an entire dwarven army into marching into dragon territory, using nothing but sleight of hand and deception. Could he do something similar here?

He turned to Armstrong. "Tell me about the enemy's general."

"Our scouts say it's the one on the skeletal beast in front of the lines. He hasn't moved since the siege began. We assume he will lead the charge."

Reggie's mind whirred. The army was massive, impossible to fight head-on. But maybe... maybe it didn't need to fight at all.

He turned back to Armstrong. "Do you have shovels?"

Armstrong raised an eyebrow. "Boy, this is a mining town. If you need a hole, we can dig you the best darn hole you've ever seen."

Reggie grinned, "Then we might have a chance."

Armstrong leaned forward. "Explain."

Reggie nodded. "First, we need to delay the attack. Have you sent an envoy to negotiate surrender?"

Armstrong scoffed. "You think those things will negotiate?"

"No," Reggie admitted. "But we don't need them to. We need time."

He turned to the sergeant. "I need a volunteer. This is dangerous, and one or all of us may not make it back."

Sergeant Miller snapped to attention.

"I'll go."

Reggie exhaled. "Alright. Here's what we're going to do..."

5

THE BATTLE OF THE DEAD: PART 2

The fortified gate of the town groaned as it cracked open, just wide enough for Reggie and the brave sergeant to step through. Beyond the threshold, they were met with a cold west wind carrying the scent of decomposition and decay. Their mission was suicidal, and they both knew it. But doing nothing was even worse. So, they walked.

Step by step, they closed the distance between themselves and the silent horde of the dead.

At the army's center, the General's massive, blackened war beast snorted, its hoofbeats pounding the ground like war drums. Smoke curled from its nostrils, and an eerie heat radiated from its body as if it had been forged in the very depths of the underworld.

Reggie fought the urge to turn and run. This was madness. Absolute madness. The skeletal archers on either side of the army raised their crossbows, fingers poised over their triggers.

Any second now…

Reggie braced himself. But no arrows came. They were letting him approach.

Only then did he realize he hadn't breathed since leaving the gate. He stopped and inhaled deeply—but it didn't help.

He took another step forward, forcing his voice to remain steady.

"Uh… General, sir," Reggie called out, his throat dry. "I am Reggie Blackstone, an envoy sent to discuss peace with you. To whom am I addressing?"

Silence.

The air hung thick and foul, pressing against Reggie like an unseen weight. He swallowed. Had he mumbled? Did the General even have ears?

Seconds dragged. Nothing.

He cleared his throat, preparing to repeat himself—louder this time.

"General, sir, I am…"

"I heard your pitiful, sterile voice the first time," the General growled.

The sound that followed was hideous. It was as if his words were being dragged through a raging fire, torn apart and reassembled in something barely comprehensible.

Reggie stiffened. That voice was not meant for human ears. But at least he could understand it. That meant there was still a chance. Reggie was taken aback, of course, but relieved that communication was theoretically possible and even more relieved that he hadn't been killed… yet.

Reggie found his voice. "So… who am I addressing?"

The General straightened, his charred skeletal form towering over them. "The gall of these people," he said, loud enough for his army to hear. "They send a mere boy to parley with the great General Lord Mortifier, ruler of the armies of the dead."

Reggie held his ground as Mortifier continued.

"Is your leader a fool? A coward? Why does he not crawl before me himself, begging to be heard?"

His barked laughter sent an unnatural reverberation across the smoky battlefield.

Reggie fought the urge to step back.

Mortifier's violet eyes burned into him. "Peace?" he spat, the word rolling like poison on his tongue. The General's laugh turned into a roar, loud enough that it could be heard even behind the city walls.

Every hair on Reggie's neck stood on end. Reggie forced himself to smirk, though his insides twisted. "Yes, your uh… deadness," he said, trying his best to sound confident.

He was thankful in one sense that Felix wasn't here. There was no telling what the talking man-bag would say right now. Sometimes Felix struggled to control his tongue. Well, the truth is, he didn't know how. He missed his friend deeply.

"For both of our well-being, I have come to negotiate peace."

Mortifier laughed harder, the sound rattling through his ribcage like a coffin lid slamming shut.

"I have fought thousands of battles in thousands of years, and never has anyone come to negotiate with me," he sneered.

He paused, his hollow sockets narrowing slightly. "Okay, I am curious. What do you bring to offer me, boy?"

Reggie could sense the fish nibbling at the hook—a little bit.

"Gold? Jewels? The wealth of your city's mines?" Mortifier scoffed. "If I take your city, I own your gold. And tell me—what use do the dead have for treasure? We do not build mansions. We do not swim in luxurious pools in the backyard. In case you were unaware..." he leaned forward, voice dripping with mockery, "skeletons cannot swim."

The undead soldiers chuckled at their General's joke. This low, rattling sound sent shivers down Reggie's spine, but he stored that notion for later.

Reggie ignored all the rhetoric. The dead were laughing. That was a good thing.

That meant they were listening.

That meant he had bought some time.

So, Reggie kept talking.

"Then tell me, Lord Rigormortis, what do you gain from this battle? What do you want?"

Mortifier sat back in his saddle, amused. "What do we want?" His voice was cold and final. "Simple. We want every man, woman and child in your city to die."

He folded his arms. "Now, let's negotiate."

Reggie's pulse slammed against his ribs. There was no emotion in the General's words. No malice, no hatred. Only inevitability. The dead had no desires. They simply were... dead.

Reggie's legs wavered. His vision blurred. He began to feel woozy. Was he going to faint and mess up his plan? No, not now, not this time. He must press on. He dug deep as heroes often do and found a new confidence and energy. He hoped it would last only a few more minutes. This was his greatest sleight of hand yet. He had to hold it together.

"Thank you for your candor, Sir Grave."

Mortifier's skeletal brow twitched faintly.

Reggie pressed on, leaning into the bluff.

"I will return the favor. We have no desire to die today. In fact, we've been preparing for this possibility for years."

The General tilted his head. "Interesting. Explain, boy."

Reggie took a bold step forward, now speaking as if he knew a secret Mortifier did not.

"Did you know—you probably do—that no race fears death more than humans? It's so true. But what if we found a way to defeat it?"

The whole army shifted, a ripple of unease moving through the undead ranks. Mortifier noticed. He did not like it.

"Our theory is that the dead," Reggie looked around, "as you know, won't die a second time. They will be no more and enter an infinity of horrible, dark and horrendously anxiety-producing nothingness. Not a nice place, I can assure you."

"Absurd. Show me proof, or I will destroy your city now."

"Okay," Reggie said, rubbing his chin. It was time to set the hook. He pointed over his left shoulder to Sergeant Miller, who was no more than 45 years old. "Do you see this sergeant beside me? He is actually 120 years old. Doesn't he look great for his age?"

Reggie lied.

Mortifier's burning sockets narrowed. For the first time, the General was thinking.

"That is no proof," he growled.

"Maybe the hook has been taken," thought Reggie. "Easy now, easy."

"Yes, well of course, you are correct," agreed Reggie. "I can see why you are the General of a bunch of dead people, I mean, with such a quick, insightful brain—or skull, or whatever."

Reggie smirked. The sergeant chuckled, barely containing himself.

Reggie noticed a shift in the General's stance. That was it. The hook had been taken, line and sinker as well.

"What are you proposing?" the General finally asked, voice dangerously calm.

Reggie smiled like a man in control.

"Simple. Let one of your lieutenants enter our city and undergo our experiment. If they survive, we surrender. If they don't..." He shrugged, holding his hands up magician-style, palms exposed, a habit he gained from doing sleight of hand on the streets. It was as if to say, "See nothing up my sleeves."

"So, what do you say? Can we get a dead volunteer?"

Mortifier leaned forward, considering. Then, after a long pause, he gestured to his aides. They whispered in an ancient, twisted tongue for several minutes. Then, finally—

"Very well."

A single skeletal lieutenant stepped forward. "Lieutenant Gestorben will accompany you."

Mortifier turned his burning gaze to the sergeant. "And your man will remain here as my hostage."

Reggie gritted his teeth. This was it. The real game had begun.

"How much time will you need for the experiment?"

Reggie put his hand on his chin as if he were calculating some equation. "I would say half an hour or so, no more than one hour. Surely you are in no rush. Death always wins; I have been told—at least so far."

As Reggie and the dead lieutenant entered the town, Sergeant Miller turned to the undead army. His voice was tense as he asked, "Can I talk to someone in charge?" His eyes darted away from the hollow sockets of the undead guards standing over him.

The skeletal warrior shoved him roughly toward General Mortifier's towering war steed, its charred black bones glistening under the blood-red sky. Mortifier's violet-burning gaze snapped toward the kneeling sergeant.

"What is it you want to say, fool?"

The sergeant's hands were tied behind his back, but his shoulders shook with something Mortifier didn't expect.

Terror. Desperation. Regret. Shame.

"I... I don't know what to do." Sergeant Miller's voice broke. His body collapsed into the dirt. "I'm afraid. I—I think this could be the end of everything—for the living... and the dead."

Mortifier's expression didn't change, but the air around him tensed. "Stop your blubbering, man. You may not be dead, but you are a soldier. Straighten up and speak sense."

The sergeant forced himself upright, but his voice was hollow. "The weapon... it's not what they think it is."

Mortifier's skeletal fingers tightened around the reins. "You mean there actually is such a thing?"

The sergeant nodded quickly, his breath coming fast. "Oh yes. I was one of its designers. It works... better than we ever imagined."

Mortifier leaned forward. "Go on."

"Your soldier won't survive it, well... you know what I mean. In only a little while, he will be sent to a place—a state where there are only cries, anguish and pain, bad unresolved jokes, even more Marvel sequels and Brussels sprouts. It is a horrific weapon. It should be destroyed."

The words hung in the air.

"And in the wrong hands," the sergeant continued, his voice dropping to a whisper, "I can't even imagine what would happen."

A pause.

"Young Reggie appears kind, but his ambitions are... unimaginable."

Mortifier's burning sockets narrowed. "You mean to say..."

"He needed to test it on the dead," the sergeant blurted out. "And you—you gave him the opportunity he could never create on his own. You fool."

He froze, realizing what he had said.

"I—I apologize, General, I meant no disrespect, please forgive me."

Mortifier didn't respond. Because at that moment, an inhuman, unearthly, blood chilling scream rose from within the fort.

It ripped through the battlefield; a sound so filled with agony that even the undead soldiers flinched. Mortifier's entire army stiffened. Even he felt it—a ripple of something he had not known in centuries. Was it... fear? How can the dead feel fear?

His eye sockets snapped back toward the sergeant. "Tell me how to destroy it."

Sergeant Miller nodded rapidly, his voice urgent. "You cannot charge the fort. You and all of your men will be permanently erased."

A long silence.

"Then what?" Mortifier asked.

The sergeant took a deep breath; his eyes filled with shame. "We are a mining town. We sit on a labyrinth of underground tunnels. Only those of us who have lived here our whole lives know the way."

Mortifier listened.

"One tunnel in particular leads straight inside the town

walls. It's unguarded. Forgotten. Send a dozen of your best warriors—no more, no less. It is a thin tunnel. I can lead them straight to the weapon's storage place. Once you have it... the town will have no choice but to surrender."

Mortifier tilted his skull a bit. "And then we destroy the weapon?"

"Yes, exactly."

A pause.

Mortifier's voice lowered. "And what do you get out of this?"

The sergeant did not hesitate.

The sergeant's plea was desperate, his voice cracking as he fell to his knees, "Spare my people," he begged.

Mortifier was silent for a long moment.

"You mean to tell me," he said slowly, "you would betray your own fort, give me the only weapon that could ever undo my armies, to save a handful of people?"

The sergeant's lips trembled, but he nodded.

"Yes."

A long pause this time. Then, finally...

"Stay here and be silent."

Mortifier strode away, gathering his commanders. Minutes passed; a decision was reached.

"Very well," Mortifier said, returning. "We accept your plan. You will lead us. But if there is any deception, you will perish, and we will find your family and make sure they suffer an unimaginable death."

"Yes, of course," the sergeant murmured. "For the good of the living... and the dead."

Mortifier turned away. The trap was set.

～

Mortifier handpicked all his top commanders, warriors who had never known defeat. Normally, he would have sent them. But this time?

For the first time in centuries, Mortifier felt the need to lead the team himself. The rest of his dead army would be under the leadership of sergeants.

Something in the back of his rotting skull told him this was bigger than a simple siege.

Sergeant Miller took the two dozen dead commanders to a bluff a couple of hundred yards to the east of the town, hidden from the sentries by a large copse of evergreen trees and boulders. As the sergeant promised, there was a thin crack between two boulders that led down to a long, thin tunnel, only wide enough for a single file. Once in the tunnel, they lit torches, and the trail became manageable. The sergeant periodically stopped to take note of the surroundings and chose one open tunnel over another and then repeated the process again and again.

At the end of one long tunnel that the General felt was finally headed in the right direction, there was a single wooden door roughly hinged to tunnel supports.

Tension was high.

"There," said the sergeant nervously. "Inside that door is an open cave, maybe 100 feet square, with another iron door that opens into the fort. No one will expect us. This passageway hasn't been used for years, and so it is undefended. The weapon is in a hut to the immediate right of the second door. Once we are in, we must rush the guards at the facility. Speed is of the utmost importance. Any questions?"

The General nodded at two of his bulkiest and strongest men, who easily opened the thick wooden doors. They found themselves inside a massive, underground, frozen cavern, eerily quiet.

"There," the sergeant whispered, pointing to a wooden door at the far end.

"Beyond that door is the weapon."

Mortifier nodded to his men, "Break it down."

His warriors rushed forward—but, at that moment, the first door exploded, and a wall of ice and stone collapsed behind them. They were trapped. Unbeknownst to them, at the last moment, the sergeant had jumped through the entrance and was spared the blast.

Just as Reggie had experienced only hours before, a sharp biting cold—a cold far beyond what any of them had ever experienced—began to penetrate their skeletal bodies. The General saw through the light of their quickly dimming torches a jagged, frozen cavern stretching endlessly in all directions. The walls were smooth ice, reflecting a warped, ghostly image of himself wherever he looked. The single iron door loomed at the far end, frost beginning to coat its surface.

"Surely, the boy doesn't think that we dead are affected by cold, does he?"

A sudden gust of frigid wind howled through the cavern. The frost on the door thickened.

This time, there was no one to suggest there might be a key that would open the strange, single iron door in front of them, which was already covered with six inches of ice, now seven, now ten.

Mortifier turned.

His dead warriors were beginning to freeze solid.

What kind of room was this? There was only a chilling silence—and another flurry of icy wind, followed by another.

Each time, another layer of ice covered everything in the cavern.

Soon, all the skeletons were frozen solid and under feet of thick ice. Still alive... uh... or dead... whatever.

The last thing the General saw was his own reflection twisting and warping in the ice.

Then, silence.

The plan worked brilliantly. Reggie wasn't totally sure if the miners could dig their way into the mysterious cold vault. It took all hands for the entire 60 minutes, but they finally located it. No one had ever heard of it before. No doubt due to Dolos' dark magic.

Another thing Reggie was unsure of was how the icy conditions would affect the skeletons. "It was a ridiculous plan," he thought to himself, "that should not have worked, but—King help us, it did."

Reggie was a little shocked to hear himself say, "King help us." Do those words mean anything anymore?

Without their General and his commanders, the rest of the army of the dead pulled away, unsure of their orders. What happened to the dead skeleton that had accompanied Reggie? Simply put, he had been tossed down a cavernous well in the center of town that was filled with 50 feet or so of water. The General was right— skeletons don't swim.

There would be no celebration or parades for Reggie. He was no longer there to see the results of the trick. Immediately transported, he landed hard, rolling onto the cold stone of the next level of the Shadowbound Quest.

Panting.

Shivering.

Yet alive.

Reggie sat for a time in the dim light, his breath still ragged from the fight, the echoes of Dolos' laughter still lingering in the air. His body ached. His mind was fraying at the edges.

The battle with General Mortifier had taken everything out of him—the bluff, the deception, the gamble that had turned the tide. The General and his commanders were now entombed in ice, locked away forever. The dead army had scattered; their purpose shattered without a leader.

Victory.

At least, that's how it should have felt. Instead, all Reggie felt was emptiness. The truth gnawed at him. The King had done nothing.

Dolos' laughter echoed once more.

"Well done, little magician. You might last longer than I thought."

Reggie pushed himself up, glaring into the empty air. "Is that all you've got?"

The gorgon's voice turned silky. "Oh, far from it. But tell me, Reggie... are you not wondering why your King has not come for you?"

Reggie's hand twitched toward his belt. The golden trial card.

He had done everything right, and the King had done nothing. Weary of this "chat" with his enemy, Reggie tried to step forward into the next unknown level, but his mind wouldn't let go.

Dolos. The gorgon who had conspired to destroy Qayeen. The monster who had nearly burned the world. And now,

Reggie had been forcibly and helplessly dragged into a vile game of Dolos' making.

"Why? The King would come for me. He had to. Wouldn't he?"

A new thought slithered into his mind, unwanted but poisonous.

What if the King left me here on purpose? What if this was a punishment for something that I had done wrong, or not done right? But what?

Dolos whispered this time, his voice curling through the darkness. "Tell me, Reggie... dear boy, are you not wondering why your King has not come for you? He sent you into my grasp, and now he does nothing. How much longer will you endure this... before you use the *Go to Trial* card?"

Reggie's hand twitched toward his belt, where the golden card lay tucked safely away. The thought had crossed his mind—repeatedly. He would not give Dolos the satisfaction.

Not yet. He quickly dismissed that last thought. Still, the silence was deafening.

What if Dolos was right?

Now it was the frog's golden eyes that glinted in the dim light, as if it knew exactly what Reggie was thinking.

"You will have to decide for yourself, Quester."

The strangling silence pressed in further. Reggie's fingers found the small golden card in his pocket. It was light, yet it felt heavier than anything he had ever held. The words "Go to Trial" shimmered mockingly. It reminded him of the high-stakes cards used in back-alley dice games—except this was not a game.

This was a weapon. And it was the only easy way out. He clenched his jaw, turning it over in his hands. It felt too real.

He looked up at the frog, Jinx. The creature's golden eyes

studied him, its throat puffing in slow, deliberate croaks. There was no mockery. No taunt. Only patience.

"It is yours to use," Jinx said, his voice smooth and careful. "At any time, you may invoke the Trial. The High Court will hear your case. You will argue that you have done nothing wrong and are being unfairly treated. You are in the right. Don't you agree? And should you succeed in convincing the judge of your case against the King, he will admit that Shadow Lord was right, you will be publicly exonerated and restored to your pathetic life."

Reggie swallowed, his mouth dry.

"And if I lose?"

Jinx blinked lazily.

"Then you return to your punishment, none the wiser. You will continue until you perish or succeed. But that is unlikely, isn't it?"

The way he said it made Reggie nauseous.

"You are already beginning to see it, aren't you?" Jinx continued, tilting his slick green head. "The silence. The absence. The King *has* abandoned you, and yet you still fight for him. Why?"

Reggie wanted to snap back, to deny it—but the words caught in his throat. Because deep down, a small, vicious voice in his head was already whispering: "Where is he?"

Reggie's hands trembled as he shoved the trial card back into his pocket.

Not yet.

Not yet.

He needed to think. This was not like the King. There must be an explanation.

But the silence around him suddenly felt louder, as if the whole world was watching, waiting. Waiting for him to break.

Reggie exhaled sharply, pushing the thought aside. He wasn't going to fall for Dolos' mind games.

Not yet.

He squared his shoulders and stood up, forced the trial card back into his pocket.

"Fine," he muttered. "Let's get this next silly level over with."

Ten more diamonds appeared on his bracelet, making 15 in all.

And somewhere, unseen, Dolos' serpentine lips turned up slightly at the edges.

6

LEVEL TWO: THE DEADMAN'S HAND

The salt spray stung Reggie's face as he jolted awake, swaying precariously atop a long, thick, wooden plank that bowed under his weight. One end rested on the deck of a massive pirate ship, the other jutted out over churning waves where massive sharks circled like hungry shadows.

Rough-looking pirates lined the ship's rail, their cruel eyes gleaming. Reggie's arms were bound tightly behind him.

This was it, the second level of Dolos' insane trial. And it looked like curtains.

A heavy footstep landed on the plank, making it groan. A burly pirate captain, his face a roadmap of weathered lines, strode forward, a gleaming cutlass raised high.

"Any last words, Bob White?" he roared.

"Bob White?" Reggie's mind raced.

"Why am I walking the plank? What did I do?" he said, stalling.

"You sniveling dog!" spat the first mate. "You snuck into the captain's quarters and tried to steal his peg leg! What kind of lowlife does that? That's worse than taking our Pop-Tarts. The penalty for such a hideous crime on the Black Mercy is to walk the plank."

The crew erupted into laughter, hooting and hollering. The captain's sword flashed in the sunlight. No more time.

Suddenly, everything froze. There was no movement, no sound and no smells.

Below the plank, in a strange, tiny dinghy, bobbed the magic frog, Jinx, the caretaker host of this bizarre game. It's funny where your mind goes at times like these. Reggie wondered how Jinx could row the boat with his pitifully small, webbed hands. He shook his head and returned to his precarious situation.

"Welcome to Level Two, boy," Jinx croaked, unfazed. He was wearing a black tricorn pirate captain's hat, though it seemed far too big for his flat, forthright head.

"Seems you survived the zombie skirmish. Too bad. We'll have to tweak the game mechanics. Regardless, you've earned your 10 diamonds. Now, your avatar is Bob White—a Caribbean boatswain's mate with a talent for tall tales and rubbing people the wrong way. The crew doesn't trust you with all your yapping about voodoo and such. They want you gone. Who knows if you did try to steal the captain's leg? Shame on you if you did."

Reggie glanced at his reflection in the captain's sword. Dark skin. Dreadlocks. Tribal tattoos. He barely recognized himself.

"Fifteen diamonds total," the frog continued. "You can keep them if you plan on surviving, or—given your current predicament—you may want to buy an item from the Shadowbound bodega. Let's see." The frog put on frog-sized glasses and held up a tiny frog-sized bag. "Hmm, your limited choices are a magic wand for 10 diamonds—unpredictable but powerful, we are not sure what it can do— or an elixir to heal a single wound, also 10. Or… a plain deck of cards for five."

Reggie hesitated. Then, surprising even himself, he proclaimed, "The deck of cards."

"Interesting choice," Jinx mused. "Most go for the wand and its wild magic. Suit yourself. The cards are in your pocket, and you are down to 10 diamonds. Good luck, Bob."

Level Two restarted abruptly.

The captain's blade hovered inches from his chest.

"Hold on!" Reggie… uh… Bob shouted, his voice no longer his own. It was Bob White's island twang.

"Cap'n, mi got a likkle proposition fi yuh—one yuh nah go waan refuse!"

Bob had no idea what it was yet. But he wasn't going down without a fight.

"One last game, Cap'n. Jus' you an' me. Wha'cha say?"

The crew murmured. A wager was sacred on the sea. Even cutthroats respected a wager. The captain chuckled, adjusting his broad-brimmed hat.

"A fool's bet, but I like a bit of sport," the captain smirked. "You'll be feedin' the fish in a minute, lad."

"Then what's di harm in one final hand? If yuh win, mi jump willingly. No fight, no fuss."

The captain leaned in. "And if you win?"

Reggie smiled. A gambler's smile. A liar's smile.

"Then yuh let mi walk free. Jus'... not this direction." He pointed over his shoulder toward the plank.

A beat of silence. The captain laughed, loud and cruel.

"Fine, lad. Let's play, mano a mano."

An upright empty grog barrel quickly became their makeshift table. Two frail wooden chairs were placed on either side. The captain sliced through Bob's wrist bindings with his cutlass. "After you, my dead-man-walking friend."

Bob (Reggie) grinned cautiously. He had bought himself time. And few were more skilled with cards than Reggie. He needed to stack the deck in his favor. But what would that look like? What's the gig?

"Someone get us a deck of playing cards that none of you bilge rats have marked up," the captain barked. To everyone's surprise, Bob pulled a fresh pack from his pocket.

"Mi treat. Yuh never know when yuh find a good game, ya know?"

The captain waved a hand. "Deal."

Bob spoke, "The game? Pirate's Four-Card. Four cards each. High hand wins. No redraws."

The crew chuckled knowingly. No one could remember ever beating the captain at four-card before. The irritating islander had sealed his lousy fate. They would see this strange lad with all his superstitious, candle-burning, chanting mumbo jumbo become shark scat yet.

With a confident flick of his wrist, Bob slid the deck from its box, the sound of the cards brushing together creating a soft, almost hypnotic rhythm. He expertly fanned them out in his hands, the edges of the cards shimmering in the sunlight as if they were made of polished silver.

The crew watched in rapt attention as he shuffled with

fluid precision, his fingers dancing over the cards in a display of skill that seemed to defy the very laws of gravity. The captain was impressed and a bit concerned. Had he underestimated the sailor? There was no stopping now. A wager was a wager.

Four-card was a favorite across the seven seas. The dealer dealt each player a single card face down. Starting with the captain, each card was turned over, revealing its identity. Then the second cards were dealt and so forth. After all the cards were revealed, the points were added up, and the winner was announced.

The cards whispered against Bob's black fingers, edges shimmering in the sunlight. The crew leaned in, eyes hungry. This was even better than watching someone walk the plank —and that would likely happen anyway. The first cards fell into place.

The captain's first card—Ace of Spades. The crew erupted. An auspicious beginning. Worth 15 points.

Bob turned his own. Eight of Hearts. Only eight points.

The captain's second card—Ace of Clubs.

The crew roared again. Their captain was very popular, and Bob, well, let's just say… was not. The captain already had a pair—a high-scoring hand. The captain did the math in his head. Fifteen plus 15 plus 10, because of the pair—40 points.

Bob casually flipped his second card. Ace of Hearts.

Now the tension grew.

The captain turned his third card. Eight of Clubs. The quartermaster shouted the tally, "48 to 23, captain leading."

Bob decided he would have some fun and play his role in a way that Felix, if he were here, would appreciate. Who knew? The act might pay off sooner rather than later. So, he

paused, rolled his black eyes back in his head, and raised his
scarred, tattooed face skyward. Holding up his gangly arms,
he cried out loud enough so that all the spirits on his home
island, far, far away, just might be able to hear him.

"Oh island spirits of mi ancestors, sea an' storm, hear
    mi cry!
Papa Dio, hide mi deep, drown bad mind in silence.
Mama Brisa, carry mi troubles 'pon de wind, blow
    dem far, far 'way.
Gran Nyoka, coil tight, strike swift, keep evil from mi
    door.
Ancesta spirits, drink dis rum, walk wid mi, guard mi
    path.
By sand, by moon, by bone—
Make dem who wish mi harm shake an' run!
So it be. So it done.
And grant me an Ace, please.
Now, it is spoken. It is done."

The pirates fell silent, many glancing at the sky to see if
anything heard.

Bob flipped his third card. Eight of Diamonds. A pair, but
not enough. 48 to 41.

The final draw. The captain reached out hesitantly and
revealed his last card.

It was the Eight of Spades.

No one spoke. No one dared to. But they all knew what
had just happened.

Bob did his best to act surprised and shocked on the
captain's behalf. But of course, he wasn't. Reggie knew
exactly what had happened.

It was the feared and cursed Dead Man's Hand. Two black aces. Two black eights. The laughter and taunting of the crew faded immediately. The air turned frigid. A superstitious hush fell over the deck.

"It's the Dead Man's Hand," someone whispered. "That's a cursed deal!"

The wind howled through the riggings. The ship seemed to groan. Shadows rapidly shifted where there should be none. The captain could only stare at his cards, his sun-scorched face drained of color. His fingers twitched. His breath came ragged. His eyes darted, expecting Death itself to step aboard.

Bob leaned in, voice smooth as rum. "What's wrong, Cap'n? Yuh look like yuh seen a ghost."

The crew backed away. Paranoia swelled. One pirate stepped forward. "You gotta set him free, Cap'n."

Another, "Or it'll be you next."

A third, "We ain't dying for you."

The captain's hands were shaking visibly, his breath shallow.

"Show me your hand," the captain barked, slamming his hand down on the barrel—maybe looking for a lifeline, a distraction, something.

Bob smirked again and slowly turned his final card. It was the Ace of Diamonds.

"Tanks be to the ancestors. Dey 'ave 'eard mi cry."

Two red aces. Two red eights. Bob had pulled the Hand of Fortune, which, any sailor will tell you, prophesies that the holder will have a good destiny—perhaps even protection from the dark spirits. Bob knew it. He had cheated Death. And it had gone even better than he had imagined.

The crew gasped. The sea had chosen. The spirits of the

oceans had clearly spoken. Now the crew must listen—or else.

"Take a lifeboat," the shocked captain muttered. "Go. Get off my ship."

Bob smiled and quickly headed to the single lifeboat. No point delaying. He had learned that when the trick was over, it was best to get off the stage. Crowds can be fickle.

The crew stepped away as if touching Bob might seal their fates as well. The sea roared beneath as he stepped into the rowboat. The captain stared blankly at his cursed hand, still in shock and disbelief, his breath ragged.

The rowboat rocked violently as Bob pushed away from the doomed ship, the sea restless beneath him. The air was thick, charged with something unseen but undeniable—as if the ocean itself had been watching, waiting.

"Frog, I need some oars. I want to buy a pair of oars, now!"

"Ribbit, hmmm, let me see, life jacket, water, hmmm, some dominoes…"

"Frog… now!"

"Ah, yes, here we are. They are well built, and so five diamonds will do."

As Bob rowed away as fast as he could, he heard the crew muttering:

"We shoulda' thrown him overboard instead."

"Ain't no luck gonna save the Cap'n now."

"The sea always collects what it's owed."

The pirate ship, the Black Mercy, loomed farther behind him, her sails snapping like the wings of a restless beast. The once-boisterous crew now stood in eerie silence, backs pressed against the railings, eyes wide with dread. No one moved. No one dared.

On the deck, the captain still clutched his chest, his breath coming in shallow gasps. The Dead Man's Hand had apparently sealed his fate—or so every soul aboard assumed.

Was it an overreaction of an overly superstitious man and crew or was something darker at play? Honestly, Bob hadn't expected such a visceral reaction. The captain looked like he might be having a heart attack.

"No, most likely an anxiety attack," Reggie thought to himself. "He would be fine in a few minutes." He would focus on getting as far away from the Black Mercy as he possibly could. He grabbed his new oars and rowed like there was no tomorrow. That might be the case.

An ominous wind howled through the rigging. The whispers slithered through the crew, fear lacing every syllable. They knew the rules of the ocean—a man marked by death does not sail for long.

Then came a simple, clear order from the captain. He had a change of heart. If he was going down to Davy Jones' Locker, then Bob was going with him.

"Blow that islander out of the water. Let's give the island spirits something to satisfy their vile thirst. It is either him or us. Prime the port cannons. Fire when ready."

The deck of the Black Mercy roared with activity as the pirates scrambled into position, their boots pounding against the worn planks. The gun crew moved with an urgency and speed that had been honed over the years. Such skills meant survival in battle—and perhaps now.

The salty wind carried the scent of gunpowder and sweat, mixing with the distant rumble of thunder on the horizon.

"Load 'em up, ye slack-livered sea rats!" bellowed the quartermaster, his voice raw with command. His cutlass gleamed under the fading sun as he pointed toward the distant dinghy, moving far too slowly across the horizon—not far enough away.

A handful of gunners, their shirts torn and stained with black powder, heaved open the cannon hatches. The iron muzzles, blackened from years of fire and fury, groaned as they were hurriedly rolled into position. Crates of cannonballs clattered as they were pried open, heavy iron spheres rolling onto the deck with deep, menacing thuds.

"Swab those barrels! Pack 'em tight! Get the lead out, boys." A grizzled gunner's mate barked, shoving a wad of dry cloth into the cannon's gullet. Another pirate, face smeared with soot, plunged a long ramrod down the barrel, twisting it to secure the gunpowder charge before stepping aside.

"Load shot!"

Two crewmen hefted a cannonball, muscles straining, and guided it into place with practiced efficiency. Another followed, packing the ammunition down tight. The deck vibrated as more cannons were loaded in unison, a deadly rhythm of steel and fire.

"Elevation! Adjust by two degrees!" shouted the master gunner, squinting through a spyglass at the lone dinghy bobbing vulnerably in the waves. "We need a clean shot— wait for the roll!"

The pirates grinned, some spitting into the sea for luck, others wiping sweat from their brows. They had done this a thousand times before. There was no honor in slaughtering a man in a rowboat—but there was amusement.

"Aim for the hull! Let's see 'im swim!"

The quartermaster raised his arm, the crew tensed, fingers hovering over the slow matches, ready to ignite the fuses.

Then—

"FIRE!"

A deafening boom shattered the evening air. Flames erupted from the cannon muzzles, belching thick clouds of white smoke as the first volley was unleashed. The ship rocked from the force of the blast, wooden beams groaning under the pressure.

The cannonballs screeched through the sky, hurtling toward the helpless dinghy with the promise of obliteration. Reggie ducked as the cannonball flew right over his dreadlocked head.

He knew they would make the needed adjustments—that's what they did. He frantically rowed away but wasn't sure if it would do any good at this point. It was a game well played, but…

A deep, low groan rumbled—not from man nor beast—but from the ship itself. Reggie paused, oars frozen in his hands. He turned back instinctively.

The hull of the *Black Mercy* trembled, shuddering as if something vast and restless coiled beneath it. The mast groaned, sails snapping wildly in the wind—though no storm had yet arrived.

The captain, still on his knees, lifted his head to the sky, his face twisted in agony.

"No…" he wheezed. "Not yet…"

But the sea does not wait.

The first wave struck like a battering ram, a towering wall

of black water rising from the depths with unnatural force. It slammed into the port side, sending crew members sprawling and tearing ropes from the rigging. The captain tried to stand —tried to run—but the second wave crashed down, driving him back onto the deck.

He gasped for breath. Then came the third wave. It rose impossibly high, blotting out the moon, swallowing the sky.

And in that wave—something moved.

Reggie's breath caught in his throat. Through the churning water, he saw it. A shape. No, several shapes. Massive. Ancient.

Scales the color of midnight, catching the glint of lantern light. Eyes like molten gold, gleaming through the dark. Sea dragons.

The first of them surged forth, its long, sinuous body slicing through the crest of the wave like a spear, its razor-finned tail whipping through the surf. Another followed, then another—three, no, four of them—beasts of the abyss, kings of the deep.

The largest reared up beside the ship, its ridged spine towering over the mast. Its fanged maw parted, releasing a roar so vast it shook the air itself, sending vibrations rattling through Reggie's bones. Another dragon spiraled around the ship, its serpentine coils gliding beneath the surface, brushing the hull like a predator testing its prey.

The Black Mercy lurched violently as one of them struck. Its mighty tail slammed into the stern, sending planks and men flying. The ship buckled, wood shrieking in protest. The captain clawed at the deck, scrambling toward the railing—but a second dragon rose from the depths, its massive jaws clamping down on the bow like a beast seizing its kill.

Reggie saw the captain's mouth open in a silent, final scream before the sea took him.

A deafening crack split the air as the ship snapped in two, its mighty hull splitting like a broken shell. The crew was flung into the abyss, their bodies swallowed by the endless, merciless deep.

Reggie sat frozen, his rowboat bobbing like a leaf on the ocean's breath. Within moments, the Black Mercy was gone. The sea stilled. The wind vanished. The world fell deathly silent. Nothing remained—no wreckage, no bodies, no trace that the ship had ever existed at all.

Reggie's heart pounded in his ears. The pirates had been right. The sea always collects what it's owed.

A single, dark shape floated to the surface—a single playing card. It drifted toward his boat, spinning lazily, untouched by the waves. Reggie leaned forward, hesitating, then plucked it from the water.

It was an Ace of Spades, the same card the captain had first drawn.

A shudder ran through Reggie's spine. He turned it over. On the back, scrawled in black ink, was a single word: "Raziel."

Immediately, Reggie knew what was happening. Who helped him? Maybe it was the Drukyl dragons? But they would likely use his real name—Reggie. That might explain the sea dragons, though. But how did they find out? Whoever it was, they wanted to send a secret message to Reggie. He took comfort in the fact that he was not alone.

He relaxed and took a deep breath. But Reggie's breath hitched. His fingers tightened around the card. The world around him blurred. The ocean, the sky, the wind—all faded into shadow.

Level Three was waiting.

And something—or someone—was watching.

A quiet, terrible thought erupted inside him: "The King *had* known. He *had* known this would happen."

Not only that—he had allowed it.

But it was the Drukyl who came to his aid. Not the King.

Could this keep up? He felt inside his pocket for the *Go to Trial* card. Though drenched in seawater, it was none the worse for wear. He realized that his fingers were rubbing the card a little too long.

"King, where are you? What did I do to offend you so? Why won't you tell me? I am innocent. Do you care? Have you ever really cared?" he cried helplessly into the foreboding sky.

7

LEVEL THREE – THE GREAT CONFLAGRATION

Reggie awoke in his own bed inside the Street Shadows warehouse. Surprised, he urgently looked around and confirmed this wasn't a dream. "No, I am home," he exclaimed to himself. "Is the game over?"

A quick glance at the bracelet on his wrist, now with 15 diamonds, removed any hope of such a thing. Reggie did a little math in his head. He had 15 diamonds at the beginning of Level Two. He spent 10 on cards and oars. But he got those 10 back by surviving the level. Fifteen.

Reggie shook his head. He felt lonelier than ever—even depressed. "But, maybe, just maybe, it is all over?" he thought.

Again, as if it could read Reggie's very thoughts, the eccentric frog leapt up on his shoulders and somberly said, "Boy, the answer is no!"

This time, the frog was wearing a bright yellow fireman's hat and a full-body slicker. He looked quite absurd to Reggie.

"So, what's the deal with the hats?" said Reggie, pointing to Jinx's head.

"Hats? Braaaap!" belched the frog, looking up to the sky. "Indubitably, I have no idea what you mean."

He went on. "There are five levels left. The two easy ones are done. Like the special forces say, 'The only easy day was yesterday.' So much more fun to come. I have to say that I am surprised. The betting line was that you wouldn't make it this far. I was as surprised as anyone that the pirates were attacked by large sea creatures. We must investigate the source of that. You are not getting help from the outside, are you? Hmmmm? Braaaap! Disqualification is very serious. You definitely don't want that."

Reggie shook his head in dismay—partly to answer Jinx's question, but partly out of discouragement that all of this hadn't been a nasty dark dream.

"So, I did bring your complaint to the King," Jinx lied. "He was surprisingly indifferent to my request for some clarity for you, boy. I will ask again when I have the opportunity. And to show you that we are not total strangers to compassion, we are giving you a respite before Level Three, allowing you to get some food and rest. Please take advantage of this truly gracious gift. There may not be another. Beware of telling anyone—anyone at all—about the game. If you do, you will immediately forfeit the game, your own life, and the lives of all you talk to about it. Is that crystal clear? Braaaap?"

"Remember, you have diamonds to spend. Let me see. For two diamonds, you can get a Scratch and Win lottery card. One diamond for a Brussels sprouts cookbook—hardly ever used. Here's a new one. For five, you can get advice from three of the wisest oracles around. Hmmm, but that deal is only good for a short time. Don't be a stranger."

With that, the frog vanished into nothingness, leaving Reggie with more questions than answers.

"What is it with that frog?" thought Reggie. "And what is with the King?"

Despite what the frog said, Reggie needed to inspect the Street Shadows warehouse to make sure no foul play had fallen upon his friends—his family.

"Hey, Reggie," huffed Buzz the dragon, "What's up? We missed you yesterday. Look, I can create smoke circles." He did so. It was impressive, thought Reggie.

"I can make big and small ones. I can even do one in the shape of a tree. I am working on a bumblebee. Hey, do you think you can use that in your street act? I mean, it is cool, right?"

"Yeah, more than cool," Reggie had to smile. He had only been gone for a day or so… how long had it been? But this was home. This was indeed family. He felt the weight of the previous day slide off his burdened shoulders.

Just then, Raoul bumped into him. Raoul was the best pickpocket he had ever seen. "Hey, boss, can I show you my latest trick? This will wow the crowd. Or I can make some side-hustle cash. So here we go."

His speech transitioned into a stage voice. "So, sir, is this your bracelet?" He held up Reggie's bracelet with the 15 diamonds high in the air and began to laugh out loud. He was joined by Buzz and some of the others.

"Hey, give that back to me," Reggie barked, a little too strongly. "Sorry, buddy," he immediately regretted his overreaction. "Okay, okay, that was pretty good, alright," agreed Reggie, retrieving the bracelet quickly with no explanation. "Hey, has anyone seen Felix?"

"Nope," said Raoul, "we thought he was with you. I mean, he's always with you. Where can a magic pouch with no legs go anyway?"

"Yeah, that's what I thought. He must be playing a trick on me."

From the small kitchen, the halfling twins, Jo-Bob and Alice, announced that their specialty—hot shrimp, ghost pepper and oyster pizza—was ready for any who dared. Reggie dared.

It was good to be home. Reggie went back to his modest room so that he could be alone and shut the door behind him.

"Frog," Reggie cried, "I want to spend some diamonds. Now, if you please."

THE THREE WISE ORACLES

Reggie stared at the so-called Oracles standing before him. He had spent five of his precious diamonds to summon them, hoping—begging—for some kind of clarity. But now, looking at them, he wasn't so sure he'd made the right choice. He noted that they cost about as much as oars—that felt about right.

The first oracle, Uphaz, was a massive elephant, his wrinkled gray skin draped in golden robes, his tusks gleaming like polished ivory. His small, wise eyes twinkled as he reached out of Reggie's window with his trunk, plucking a tuft of long grass from the ground. He placed it between his teeth and chewed slowly, like every bite carried the weight of deep contemplation.

The second oracle, Belyadad, was a shaggy old dog of some unknown breed or combination of breeds, his fur matted with age, his nose twitching as if he were sniffing for half-eaten leftovers instead of divine wisdom. He sat, panting lazily, his tail thumping against the dirt.

The third oracle, Sippor, was a big old magpie—a twitchy,

sharp-eyed, sharp-tongued black-and-white bird that wouldn't stop frenetically hopping back and forth. She fluffed her feathers, glaring at Reggie like she was waiting for the chance to tell him he was an idiot.

Reggie folded his arms. "Alright, wise oracles, I need answers. The King won't talk to me, no matter how much I call out. So, tell me—is all this a punishment? What have I done? I feel like I have been faithful to the King. Why am I going through this? It seems so unfair, unjust? I'd rather not take the King to court to find out. So, tell me."

Uphaz, the elephant, let out a deep, thoughtful rumble as he chewed, the crunch of grass filling the silence. "Oh, young traveler," he said finally, swishing his tail, "you seek wisdom, yet wisdom must first find you worthy. No one has been closer to the King than I. No one has heard his voice more clearly. Do you know what he has told me?"

Reggie leaned in, desperate. "What? What did he say?"

"That I am a most excellent servant," Uphaz said proudly, puffing out his chest. "And that I am truly wise."

Reggie blinked. "That's it?"

"Indeed!" the elephant boomed, plucking another piece of grass with his trunk. "For you see, my people—the great elephants of Teman—are the keepers of wisdom! We study it, we teach it, we share it freely. But wisdom is only for those who are truly wise enough to receive it. So, tell me, young one, are you wise?"

Reggie clenched his fists. "I don't know, that's why I'm asking you!"

Uphaz chuckled, his massive ears flapping. "Ah, but see, the fact that you do not know means you are not."

Reggie groaned. "Are you serious right now?"

Uphaz ignored him and continued, his trunk swaying as he

spoke. "I received a message for your ears last night, a whisper from the throne room itself. It came to me in a dream —no, a nightmare. A shadow passed over me, its voice like cold wind on my tusks, and it said:

'How can any human claim to be truly faithful? Only the King is faithful. Look at your suffering. Look at your pain. Clearly, you have been found unworthy, and this punishment is just.'"

Reggie felt like he'd been punched in the stomach. "Punishment? But I didn't *do* anything wrong!"

Belyadad, the dog, gave a lazy stretch, yawning so wide that Reggie could see all his teeth. "Aww, kid, that's what they all say," he said with a deep southern drawl, his tail wagging. "Listen, I've served the King for *ages*—longer than this wrinkly old elephant here."

"That is *highly* debatable," Uphaz muttered.

Belyadad ignored him, shaking out his stiff, mangy fur. "And lemme tell ya somethin', boy—this ain't complicated. The King don't punish people for *no reason*. If you're suffering like this, you *must've* messed up. Big time. Innocent people are as rare as Phoenix tears and not as helpful."

Reggie threw up his hands. "I paid five diamonds for worn-out, stupid clichés and platitudes?"

[Storyteller's Note: Far-fetched stories of the Phoenix bird are fairly common throughout Garden City and Amaratzim, though the fact of the matter is that no one I know has ever seen one. It is a mythical bird that has regenerative properties of some kind—though every new yarn describes its properties differently. Most children's stories feature a character being reborn after it has burst into flames. No one is sure why it

might cry—or how anyone could collect a tear. Or what that tear might be able to do, if... if... if. So "That's as rare as a Phoenix tear" is an overused saying, the equivalent of "That's rare as a Brussels sprout side dish that tastes good...." or "That's as rare as a Marvel sequel worth seeing." You get the idea, back to Reggie.]

"Tell me what I did!" Reggie blurted out to the mangy oracle.

Belyadad sniffed at the air. "Dunno. Maybe you forgot to bow low enough? Maybe you didn't say 'thank you' after a blessing? Maybe you—oh, I dunno—committed *high treason* and didn't realize it?" He scratched behind his ear.

"But whatever it was, it had to be *bad*. Because, trust me, the King does *not* reject people who are faithful. If you were as good as you claim to be, you wouldn't be here. No, you would be on a great and honorable quest. That is where the favored children of the King go—not this travesty."

Reggie's blood boiled. "So let me get this straight. If you're *not* suffering, that means you're faithful. And if you *are* suffering, that means you're guilty—no matter what?"

Belyadad's tail swished like a drunk metronome. "Now you're gettin' it, kid. Maybe you are wise after all?"

Reggie gritted his teeth. "So, you're saying that because *you're* not being tortured right now, that automatically means you're righteous?"

"Exactly! That is a great self-evident point," the dog said cheerfully, stopping to scratch his hind quarters the way dogs do. "The law is the law! Good dogs get treats. Bad dogs get the leash. Same with the King. Good servants get honor. Bad ones get the whip."

Reggie screamed. "BUT I AM INNOCENT! I DON'T DESERVE ANY OF THIS!"

Belyadad gave a pitying look. "Mmm. Yeah, see, that's what *guilty* people say."

His ears perked up. His nose twitched. In an instant, all his grand wisdom was forgotten.

"WAIT... is that..."

Without another word, Belyadad bolted out of Reggie's window, barking wildly as he took off after a rabbit that had darted out from behind a bush.

"GET BACK HERE!" Reggie shrieked. "I paid five diamonds for your thoughts."

But the old dog was already gone, tearing through the underbrush like a mad dog, yapping like his life depended on it. A few moments later, they heard a *thud*, a *yelping*, and then... silence.

Suddenly, the magpie swooped down from a tall cabinet, her sharp beak now only inches from Reggie's face.

"Oh, ENOUGH with this nonsense!" Sippor shrieked as she fluttered her brilliant white-and-black plumage. It was a piercing, earsplitting shriek, a sound so sharp it sliced through the air like jagged glass. It wasn't only loud—it was unnatural. The pitch was so high it sent a stabbing pain through Reggie's eardrums, causing him to cover his ears with his hands. Uphaz intentionally flapped his huge, grey ears down as well.

"You wanna know the truth, boy?" She screeched again, tilting her head at him. "You dare to say, *oh, woe is me! I am so faithful! I am so righteous! Why am I suffering like this?*" She let out another shrill laugh. "HAH! You should be grateful the King hasn't truly punished you yet. If he gave you what you *actually* deserved, you'd be begging for Dolos to take you back!"

Reggie's thoughts whirled. "What... what are you talking about? I *have* been faithful! He knighted me a little while ago."

Sippor cut him off with another piercing squeal. "Oh, you *think* you're faithful, but what do *you* know of faithfulness? If he's allowing this to happen to you, it means you deserve it! Everyone gets what they deserve—nothing more, nothing less."

Reggie clenched his jaw. "That's not true."

"Oh, isn't it?" Sippor taunted, quieter this time. "Then why is the King silent?"

And that hit deeper than it should have, because the King *was* silent. Reggie swallowed hard. Maybe the oracles weren't here to help him; maybe this was part of the game. And maybe... just maybe... Dolos wasn't the only one playing it.

Reggie woke the next morning to find his world in flames.

Screams ripped through the night, tangled with the roar of the flames as the docks of Buzah City were helplessly consumed by a raging inferno. The fire had already devoured parts of the Street Shadow warehouses—the sanctuary Reggie built from nothing, the home for kids with nowhere else to go. Chaos and screams filled every direction.

The blaze seemed to be a living entity, a ravenous, bad-tempered beast that clawed at his skin.

Its smoke coiled into his lungs, choking him as he stumbled out of his room into the warehouse. The structure groaned around him; charred beams trembled, moments from collapse.

He forced himself forward. All he could think of was that it was up to him—he had to save the others.

The acrid air scorched his throat as he pushed deeper, shielding his face against the searing heat. It wasn't the flames reaching upward; it was fear itself clawing at him, whispering in the back of his mind, "You can't do this. You're going to die here."

He shoved the thoughts down. Not today. Not them.

He raised his arms, shielding his face, though the heat penetrated everything. The charred wood groaned beneath his feet, threatening to give way at any moment. He stumbled, nearly falling, but caught himself on a splintered beam.

He could barely see a foot in front of him. The flames licked at his clothes, and he could smell the singed fabric. He knew he couldn't stay here long. The air was too thick, the heat too intense, and the oxygen already burned away.

He pressed on, deeper into the inferno. The abominable sounds of the fire were deafening: the crackling, the roaring, the hissing. It was a foul symphony of destruction, a chorus of despair. He could hear the screams of the trapped from all directions, their voices muffled by the flames, their cries for help lost in the chaos.

He desperately scanned the surroundings, searching for any sign, any clue as to what he should do. But there was nothing. Just fire. Everywhere, fire. He was too late. He could feel his strength waning, his resolve faltering. He was about to give up—to succumb to the flames—when his fiery world froze.

The flames halted midair; their flickering tendrils suspended in time. The screams choked off into silence. Smoke hung motionless, like a shattered painting.

And on his shoulder, a familiar weight. Jinx.

Reggie didn't even need to look.

"Boy," said the magic frog, still in his fire gear, casually—strikingly calm in contrast to the deathly scene—his golden eyes unblinking. "This is your Level Three Trial: The Great Conflagration."

Reggie's pulse pounded against his skull. He tried to process, but Jinx didn't give him the time.

"It's all too bad, really," Jinx continued, his voice calm, unshaken. "So many people depended on you. Kids who began to turn their lives around. Kids who had nothing, and now, even less."

Jinx tilted his head, as if amused by Reggie's frustration.

"And let's not forget—you're in danger too."

Then, the dagger twisted.

"I would remind you…" Jinx gestured toward his wrist.

"The bracelet. Ten small diamonds. Each one, a lifeline. Each one, currency in this cursed game."

"You can buy one item from the store," Jinx announced with a grin.

"For five diamonds, your options are as follows: a magic wand, but, like I've said before, no one knows what it does. It could be powerful, could be useless. A coil of rope, simple and unremarkable. Last but not least… ooh, look, a wild card. With it, you can ask for anything you want. It will cost you seven diamonds. See how gracious we are? I am surprising even myself."

Jinx leaned in, his grin slow and sharp.

"Tick-tock, Player," he drawled. "Time's a-wasting, even when it's standing still."

Reggie had only seconds. Perhaps it was already too late. Reggie's mind whirled. He moved to a corner of the still and silent warehouse with the least obvious smoke—for now.

"The wand's too risky," he thought. "It could summon a tidal wave and drown everyone. Or it could turn them all into chickens. There's no time to gamble on something unpredictable."

"The rope could save me, maybe one or two others. But not all of them. And if attackers are waiting outside, they'll finish off the survivors anyway."

"The wild card, that must be it. But what? What can put out the fire, protect the warehouse and keep the Shadows safe?"

His mind went blank. He had no idea whatsoever. The game—and more importantly, his family—had lost.

"Curse this game."

Reggie closed his eyes, trying to block out the pressure, the screams trapped in time, the weight of Jinx's gaze. He focused on the feel of the diamonds against his skin, the cool smoothness a stark contrast to the burning chaos surrounding them. He thought of all the Street Shadows, the troubled teens, his friends who joined him in building this warehouse. Their faces flashed through his mind: Raoul, insecure, daddy-issued teen, but the best pickpocket in Qayeen. Fritz, the kindest giant ever. Reggie had never figured out how he could sleep so much. The halfling twins, Jo-Bob and Alice, and, of course, Buzz, the young dragon that had helped fool the dwarves and all the rest. He had let them down. He couldn't save them.

Maybe that was the whole point. Maybe this level was

designed for him, or anyone, for that matter, to lose. What if he was always meant to fail?

Reggie's hands shook—not from fear, but from rage.

"King, where are you?" he demanded of the sky. "What kind of King lets his people burn? What kind of good ruler watches His followers suffer and does nothing?"

His fingers curled into fists, his knuckles bone white.

"You are letting this happen."

"You knew this was coming, didn't you?"

"You could have stopped this before it even started. But you didn't."

His grip tightened around the *Go to Trial* card.

"Maybe Dolos was right."

"Maybe this whole game—this whole quest—was a revelation of the King's true nature."

"Maybe it was time for someone to make Him answer for it. Maybe it was time for justice. For revenge." His jaw clenched. His lips parted. He was about to call for Jinx, demand the trial begin...

A bizarre thought popped into his head.

"Wait a minute!" Reggie said, channeling his inner Felix. "It's crazy... but what the heck."

"Frog... Phoenix tear. I want a Phoenix tear."

Jinx froze. His golden eyes widened.

"What did you say?" asked the frog incredulously. "You want a what?"

"The wild card—and a Phoenix tear, now."

"Ahem, well, this is out of the ordinary," said the yellow-clad frog, his big eyes now furrowed. "I mean, the store only has practical things... You know... real things. I am not even sure where to find..."

"You said anything, didn't you? Phoenix tear now, or this

game is over," growled Reggie. "You tell your idiot boss that. Rules are rules. Phoenix tear, now."

A long pause.

With a deep, reluctant croak, Jinx's long, thin tongue extended—and, resting at its tip, a shimmering, large, tear-shaped drop of what appeared to be liquid fire.

Reggie couldn't believe it. His bluff had been called. *"There really was such a thing?"* He had hoped to throw the whole game sideways. But there it was—whatever it was—on the vile frog's tongue. He snatched it before the frog could change his mind.

The Phoenix tear sat in his grime-streaked palm, pulsing with impossible light. It looked like fire arrested mid-dance; a flame suspended inside a perfect sphere. Tiny embers twisted and turned within, casting flickers across his fingers. And yet, it was cold. Not just cool—but *cold*, like stone in a shaded crypt. A contradiction in every sense. Reggie couldn't tell if it was comforting or terrifying. Maybe both.

"Here goes nothing," he thought. Of course, the droplet didn't come with instructions, but Reggie didn't hesitate, hurling it to the ground.

The tear exploded in unimaginable light—not fire, but pure energy, which rushed outward in all directions like concentric waves.

Reggie cried out, shielding his eyes, but it was no use. The light penetrated his eyelids and seared his vision. He felt a surge of energy coursing through him, raw and powerful, like a thousand volts of electricity. He was helplessly thrown backward, landing hard on the charred planks. Then, as quickly as it began, it was over.

The flames didn't merely go out—they retracted, as if someone was rewinding time. Charred wood rebuilt itself. Ash dissolved. Smoke vanished into nothing.

The kids, once coughing and near collapse, drew in clean, fresh air at last. Their burns healed instantly. The warehouse stood strong again, as if untouched by the attack.

Reggie finally smiled, a reaction he hadn't experienced for a long time. He knew precisely what his pal, Felix, would say: "Man, I've got to get me one of those."

Outside the dock complexes, the masked arsonists stood watching their fires die. They had come expecting destruction —but what they witnessed was impossible. One of them stumbled back.

"That's... that's not natural."

Another soldier bolted. "No way we're fighting that. I'm out!"

Within moments, the attackers scattered, their fear turned into full retreat. They knew better than to challenge someone who reversed a firestorm. Dolos wasn't paying them enough to stick around.

Even Jinx grinned—or at least it looked like it—and for the first time, seemed to approve. "Well, well. Not bad, Player. Level Three: complete. You get 10 more diamonds. You are back up to 13."

Reggie exhaled, his heart still hammering. But he didn't smile. Reggie could only wonder. He had come very close to taking the King to court. If he had offended the King, it was only fair to know exactly what he had done. Was he wrong to consider it? He knew this was Dolos' plan all along, but did that necessarily make it the wrong choice?

"And where was the King? Why wasn't he here? Why didn't he speak? Why? Did I mean so little to him? Was I another pawn?" He would have to think about it later—if he even had a later. For now, there were other troubling questions.

And then, a deeper chill ran down his spine.

"If Level Three was this hard… what was waiting for him in Level Four?"

Before he could react, the world began to dissolve once more, fading into its familiar void of starless silence and colorless oblivion. As it had before, the familiar unraveling—color bleeding away, sound muffled into a vacuum, the sensation of being pulled downward.

But this time, it was different. This time, the silence was not empty. It was listening—watching.

It made Reggie's skin crawl.

He tried to move, but his body felt weightless, suspended

in an ocean of nothingness. Then, a voice, soft, whispering, right beside his ear. A different whispering voice—all too familiar.

"You were right to doubt."

Reggie jerked, but he couldn't turn, couldn't find the source.

"He *has* abandoned you."

"Who? Who has abandoned me?" he asked.

A chill raced through his veins.

"You will not survive Level Four."

The voice laughed, low and knowing. Reggie's stomach dropped. His world lurched. He was falling again.

8

LEVEL FOUR – THE TRIAL OF SHADOWS

Reggie hit the ground hard, rolling onto damp stone. His lungs heaved as he gasped for air, his entire body aching from the impact.

His vision swam. It was dark. Not just the absence of light, this was a consuming, unnatural darkness, one that pressed in from all sides, thick and tangible, as if the shadows themselves were alive and unhappy.

A single torch flickered in the distance. Beyond it, nothing but a vast, yawning abyss. No sound, no smell. Just emptiness incarnate. Jinx landed beside him with a graceful hop, adjusting himself as if he had fallen through the same eternal nothingness. This time he was inexplicably decked out in an old doctor's head mirror and a stethoscope so long it dragged along the ground, looping once around his foot.

Reggie squinted. "Really, dude? What's with the new… uh… accessories?"

Jinx adjusted the mirror with great dignity. "Ah, surely I've no idea what you mean," he croaked slightly and tilted his wet, oily head, stretching like he'd just woken from a nap.

"Anyway, welcome, my good lad, to Level Four: The Trial of Shadows."

Reggie took note of the slightly different tone of Dr. Jinx. That might come in handy down the road... if there was a "down the road."

Even though he felt a sharp pain in his left rib area, Reggie forced himself to sit up, his mind still spinning. "What is this place?" he asked, his voice hoarse and his head aching.

Jinx hummed thoughtfully, his golden eyes gleaming. "This, dear Quester, is the Trial of Shadows. A place of illusions and clarity, truth and deception, and—if you're not careful—you may lose yourself entirely."

Reggie's breath was still ragged, his heart pounding. He had barely survived Level Three. He wasn't ready for this. He was still trying to remember the identity of the voice. Was it a threat or a warning?

A low, guttural growl echoed from the darkness. Something was moving in the abyss. Something waiting. Reggie's pulse slammed against his hurting ribs.

Jinx's grin widened, his thin tongue shot out, targeting nothing that Reggie could see.

"I do hope you're ready, boy."

"What... no... I'm not ready. Let me catch my breath, I..."

The shadows surged forward. His world collapsed back into blackness. Not the simple absence of light, but a darkness so complete it pressed against Reggie's skin, thick as smoke, heavy as stone. He tried to move. His limbs felt weightless, detached. The sensation of falling wrapped around him, yet there was no air rushing past, no ground to hit. Just the abyss. No up or down, right or left. Only disorientation.

Then a whisper: "Reggie."

It was a voice he recognized. Not Jinx's. It was not Dolos'. It was a woman.

"Mom?" Reggie's breath hitched just as the void spit him out.

Reggie landed hard a second time, skidding across cold stone. He groaned, pushing himself up, his breath still uneven. "Mom? Are you there? Mom?" Nothing.

The air was thick with fog, swirling like ghostly tendrils across the ground.

He saw them. Mirrors. Hundreds of them, maybe more. Each stood tall and unbroken, stretching endlessly in all directions. They reflected nothing—not the dim light, not the fog, not even Reggie.

Dr. Jinx hopped beside him, landing lightly on a shard of broken glass.

"As I said a moment ago, welcome Player to the Trial of Shadows," the frog drawled, golden eyes flickering, his head mirror reflecting the many other mirrors.

"Wait, where's my mom? I heard her voice. Is she…?" Reggie muttered, his pulse still racing.

Jinx's throat swelled in a slow, deliberate croak.

"Braaap. If I were you, I would focus on the present. This is where your real battle begins."

A whisper curled through the fog. Reggie stiffened.

The mirrors—once empty—came alive. Before him, the glass shimmered, rippling like water.

And then—he saw himself.

Smaller. Ten years younger. The night his world fell apart.

[Storyteller's Note: You can read the whole story in "The Tale of the Orphan Magician."]

. . .

In the mirror, he saw himself in the principal's office with his parents, being scolded by the nasty man. Next he appeared in his home, in the bathroom with his terrified mother, as armed men knocked their front door down and crushed the skull of his defenseless father with an automatic weapon of some sort. Now, he was running with his mother to a nearby church, hiding in a secret vault—no, it was a secret place in a moving cart. Next, he saw the priest lying on the ground, dead. It was a twisted, confused collage of his last moments with his parents.

The scene rapidly shifted to his mother screaming at him though the mirror, "Too slow."

Reggie's hands curled into fists. "Mom? What? What do you mean?"

"Too weak."

He saw his younger self stumble, legs giving out beneath him.

"You didn't help us in time. We needed a strong son. Not you."

Then his father appeared, blood running down his face, his eyes hollowed, not real, empty. "Where was the King?" he cried. "Why wouldn't He save us?"

Reggie's breathing was shallow now, his chest tightening.

"You know the truth, don't you?" said the reflections of both of his parents in unison.

"If the King really cared, he would have stopped it."

The memory shattered, and Reggie gasped as if he'd been drowning. He was standing now, with no memory of when that happened. He put his hands on the mirror, begging for his parents to reappear.

Another mirror lit up, causing Reggie to stagger back. This time, it was not a child that stared back at him, but a young man—him—cloaked in armor, kneeling before the throne of the Great King.

It was the day he had been knighted. The moment he had sworn loyalty, honor and trust to the regent. He watched as the King smiled at him—a fatherly smile—his hand resting gently on Reggie's shoulder.

"I am so proud of you, Reggie... this time," he said.

For so long, those words had been an anchor for Reggie, a reminder that he was seen, that he was wanted, that someone had his back. But wait... what did he mean by "this time?" He didn't recall the King saying that. How had he missed it?

The images warped as if seen through an old carnival mirror. Reggie's reflection twisted toward him awkwardly.

"Was it honor?" Mirror-Reggie said, his head tilted. "Or was I only useful to the Great King?"

His gut tightened.

Reggie's reflection in the horrid mirror continued. He was no longer sure if it was the reflection or himself speaking. "You were an unwanted orphan. A street rat. He made you a knight, and you followed Him without question. You were so desperate to belong, you never stopped to wonder if it was all real. Or if he might get tired of you and cast you off at the first offense."

Now the King's warm gaze turned cold in the reflection. Mirror-Reggie continued: "He knew we would be loyal, knew we would serve him without question. What if we were merely pawns, just like everyone else who had trusted the King in the past?"

Then the mirror cracked with a pop!—shards flying in every direction.

Reggie's chest tightened, his breath becoming shallow. An anxiety attack was coming on, a sensation he hadn't felt since the days following his parents' assassination.

"Was any of that true?" he thought, taking deep, long breaths—in and out, in and out. "Had he been so eager for love that he had followed blindly?"

The third mirror flickered this time.

Jinx hopped toward it, his golden eyes knowing.

"This one's important, Player. This one must be heard," the frog murmured.

Reggie hesitated. The glass shifted. It was Dolos staring back at him. The gorgon's piercing, yellow, bulbous eyes were filled with fire and cunning.

"You think I'm the villain," Dolos said smoothly. "I get that."

Reggie stiffened. "Breathe... in... out."

"But what if I am the one telling the truth?"

The mirror warped, showing the Great King's throne room again. The King sat there in silence, unmoved, watching—as if he didn't have a care in the world.

"There he is my boy. Your hero." Dolos' reflection stated with what seemed like a tinge of compassion. "You call, but he does not answer. The King has said nothing. Done nothing."

"Magician... Reggie, you are stronger than he ever allowed you to be," Dolos said calmly and persuasively. "Please join me, and we will bring down his deceptive, narcissistic throne together."

The reflection swirled, this time showing Dolos standing before a great army, not as a tyrant, but as a liberator.

"The King has never fought for you, Reggie. But I will."

This mirror shattered like the rest.

The fog rushed back in—suffocating, drowning.

Then silence. Emptiness. Meaninglessness. Blankness.

He fell to the ground as the anxiety attack began once more like a small earthquake in his narrow chest. His fingers curled into fists without him meaning to, his palms damp, his throat tight. The world around him didn't slow down; it sped up. His heart thudded against his ribs, faster than it should, like it was trying to outrun something invisible. He couldn't breathe again. Not really. He tried, but each breath felt too shallow or too thick, like he was sucking air through cotton. His vision narrowed to the ground in front of him, to his own scuffed boots, to the tiny stone his toe kept tapping as if it were the only real thing left. He squeezed his eyes shut. It didn't help. He didn't know how long it lasted. Maybe a minute. Maybe more. But when it finally broke—when the rush of panic receded like a wave—he felt hollowed out. It was as if someone had scraped all the wholeness out of him and left only the shadow. The King had been silent. Dolos had given him answers. Was it all a lie? Was everything a made-up story? Was this trial not meant to defeat him, but to make him see? Was he truly a blind pawn of a selfish King?

"Mom?"

Reggie finally noticed Jinx watching him carefully.

"You're thinking about it, aren't you?" the frog murmured.

"Thinking about what?" Reggie rasped.

Jinx's golden eyes gleamed. "Taking the King to court to get some answers."

Reggie realized that his hand was touching the Go to Trial card. Actually, the card was entirely in his grasp.

"You are wondering, aren't you, if the Trial of Shadows was designed to make you see the truth? Or maybe it is just another lie. How do you know? Braaap!"

The frog was right, of course. Reggie was no longer confident about the King, or where he stood. And somewhere in the darkness, Dolos smiled once again.

Reggie sat for a long time in the cold darkness, his head aching and his heart racing, his mind an unbearable tangle of doubts. For the first time in his life, he felt truly isolated and alone.

His fingers brushed against his diamond bracelet. He looked down. Ten more diamonds had appeared. Now he had 23 diamonds left.

A new thought struck Reggie. "Felix!" He had enough to bring back his best friend, but it would cost him 15 diamonds, leaving him with only eight. His safety net would be largely gone. Yet, he didn't hesitate for even a moment.

"Jinx," Reggie croaked, voice raw from emotion.

The frog blinked, tilting his head, expecting that Reggie was going to play the trial card. "Yes, Player?"

"I want my friend."

Jinx's golden eyes flickered with something unreadable.

"Really? Fascinating. You humans never cease to surprise me. Fifteen diamonds then."

Reggie gritted his teeth and pulled the gems free, dropping them into Jinx's waiting, tiny, webbed hand.

The frog studied them for a second, then swallowed them whole with a loud gulp.

The air shimmered.

A familiar electric crackle filled the void.

"What's shaking, dude?"

The voice hit Reggie like a wonderful jolt to the chest.

A lump rose in his throat.

Hanging at his belt—just as he always had been—was Felix, the magic talking pouch.

The stitched mouth curved into a knowing grin, his leather form sagging slightly as if stretching after a long nap.

"Miss me?" Felix asked. "That will teach you to take me off your belt. I was going to go out and look for you, but two things stopped me: no legs, and no eyes."

Before he could stop himself, Reggie grabbed Felix and embraced him tightly.

"Whoa there, buddy," Felix said, surprised. "Did I miss something? Are we having an emotional moment? You know I don't do those, right?"

Reggie let out a choked laugh.

"Yeah. You do."

"So, hey, I've been meaning to talk with you," quipped Felix. "I've got a great idea for a new act. So, you dress up like you were a real magician, and I will..."

"Wait, what do you mean, like I was a real magician? I am a real magician."

"Well, yeah, sure, sure. I mean, quote-unquote, 'real' magician, but you know, like one on Kingdoms Got Talent."

"I could be on KGT anytime I want to. I've been too busy, you know, defeating skeleton armies of the dead, trolls... and remember the pirates?"

"Skeleton what? Okay, okay, I'm trying to read between the lines. You're begging for a pat on the back. You remember, I don't have arms either, right? Just this unending, remarkable charm and exact comedic timing. Yeah, I'm into skeleton armies as much as the next man-bag, but they aren't terribly funny or in demand right now. People are more into disappearing aardvarks. Look, I'm the brains in the act. You must work a little harder on making medium-sized animals disappear. I'm talking big time. So, check out my new idea. I put you in a big old vat of chocolate milk, with a blender, an emu, bow and arrow, and... uh... a grapefruit. Wait, note to self, maybe llamas are funnier. Well, you see, and..."

Reggie stopped listening right after "chocolate milk and blender." He missed his best friend Felix so much. "So, buddy, we need to talk."

Reggie told Felix in great detail all that had happened in the last few days.

"So, what you're saying is that I am only worth 15 tiny diamonds? It's outrageous."

"Felix, c'mon, this is serious. What do I do?"

"Well, first, we man-bags have a saying," quipped Felix. "If you are going to face an army of the undead, don't forget to bring the man-bag."

"Duly noted. I will keep that in mind next time. But what about right now?"

"Yeah, that's the question," said Felix, finally becoming serious. "What is going on with the King? This isn't like him. In fact, it is a cognitive dissonance, yeah?"

"A what?" asked a surprised Reggie. "A pretty big word for a pouch, isn't it?"

"First of all, I am a man-bag. Second, it's a little-known fact that I read very widely."

Reggie's eyes scrunched together. "Wait, how can you... never mind. I don't want to know."

"So, here's my thinking. If I can get the King into a courtroom, I can finally ask him for an explanation. He would have to answer my questions about why I am being punished. What did I do to deserve this?"

"Maybe. It's a bit of a dangerous gambit. I mean... the

King on the stand? What could possibly go wrong?"
questioned Felix.

"Yeah, that's what I thought too."

As Level Five loomed ahead, Reggie finally felt ready to face
whatever came next, because this time, he wasn't facing it
alone. He would figure out the King thing later. For now, he
needed to survive this wretched game. Somehow. Only eight
diamonds.

"King help us," he said reflexively, then thought better.
"Maybe we must help ourselves."

Dolos nodded to the behatted frog and said with no concern
whatsoever, "It's time."

"The Others? Braaap!" croaked the personality-diminished
amphibian.

"Indeed," said Dolos, his tail sweeping behind him in
excitement.

9

LEVEL FIVE: THE OTHERS

The moment Reggie materialized into Level Five, he felt it—a suffocating weight, pressing against his chest like invisible chains. The air was stifling with something unseen—some deleterious force stretching the gray, lifeless sky into an unbroken expanse of dull clouds that smothered the horizon.

We've all been there. You walk into a room full of people, and suddenly, you feel like you are confined, no way of escape, only an oppressive presence that consumes all the space. Every conversation seems taxing, laced with tension, criticism, or the looming threat of conflict, leaving no room for lightness, humor or ease. The Others in the room muscle for attention, while you feel the need to shrink away. There's nowhere to run and hide, no room to be yourself. The endless draining leaves you gasping for the air you can never quite reach.

Ahead lay such a village for Reggie and Felix. From outside eyes, it was a village slumped in decay. Wooden houses sagged under time's weight, their walls warped, their windows gaping like empty, accusing eyes. The cobbled streets were slick with a damp, lingering scent of rot and something sour—like old regret—seeping from the ground itself.

And then, the whispers from the Others began. The pointing, giggling, and finally outright mockery—all in cockney accents, of course. All Others sounded like they were from the East End within earshot of the Bow Bells.

"Look at 'im. Finks 'e's somethin' special, 'e does."

"Prob'ly a bleedin' fraud."

"Looks weak, that one. Bet 'e wears 'is tie to bed like a right ponce."

"Maybe, but look, 'es got a cute little baggie on 'is belt. I've seen better pouches on street rats."

Reggie stiffened. Felix whipped around, indignant.

"Man-bag, idiot! You've seen better *man-bags* on street-rats."

"Good one, Felix. That'll show him," Reggie muttered under his breath.

"Hmmm, looks like an old Naugahyde fanny pack and a wool bowler bag got together and 'ad a child."

"I'll have you know that my mother was a model for Dior," cried Felix defensively. It was a bad move.

One female Other huffed with disgust and sarcasm. "Oi, don't get your threads all in a knot. They must be so proud of you, dearie."

The disparaging voices slithered from everywhere—from crooked doorways, from shadowed alleys, from people who weren't even looking at him. It was a relational minefield.

The Others didn't appear monstrous on the surface. They resembled ordinary villagers in some ways—perhaps a little larger, a little more worn and wrinkled, maybe sadder. Their tattered clothing looked like something scavenged from a second-hand shop within the ruins of a world long forgotten. You wouldn't see the Others gracing the cover of Vogue anytime soon.

But something was off about them. The way their mouths curled into permanent sneers. The way their eyes held no warmth—only suspicion, judgment and quiet malice. Some adjectives that described the Others? Reproving. Unkind. Thoughtless. Unempathetic. Unaware. Disparaging. Debbie Downers. Self-righteous. Just plain critical and judgmental.

Reggie took a cautious step forward. He was too proud to walk away. Immediately, a hunched man spat at his feet.

"Oi, you're walkin' all wrong, mate."

A woman, arms crossed, scoffed. "Look at that barnet on the tall one—all floppy and uncombed. Tryin' too 'ard, ain't ya?"

A child, no older than eight, snickered, "Looks proper lost, that one. Bet 'is bloody parents made a run fer it."

Reggie clenched his fists. He had faced death, fire, cursed pirates and monstrous creatures from the abyss—but this? This was different. This was deep, internal poison. Not a quick death, not a violent one—but something slow, creeping, insidious. A venom that burrowed deep into the bones, unraveling the soul thread by thread. Every insecurity, every buried fear, was being targeted, throttled, and then dragged into the light and fed upon.

The whispers deepened, becoming even sharper, more precise.

"No wonder the King legged it. I 'eard you forgot 'is bloody birthday."

"How'd they know about the King?" thought Reggie.

"Well, I 'eard tha' this one wasn't invited anyway. Tha' 'ad to leave a mark, I must say."

"They knighted you? Pffft. What a joke. Knights ain't wot they used to be, that's for sure."

Reggie's chest tightened. His pulse pounded. His breath came quicker. Why did this feel so personal? Because—it was. Every doubt, every failure, every fear he had locked away was now being spoken aloud. His parents. The King. The people he had let down. His own worth. He feared that the King had tossed him out like trash.

His hands trembled. Fight? Flight? Freeze? No choice was safe. If he fought, they would mock his anger. If he ran, they would call him a coward. If he froze, they would tear him apart piece by piece with their words.

It was a vicious trap with no escape. What weapon would help?

Reggie's breath shook. "Felix, I need you, man. This place…"

Felix looked around, taking in the surroundings with an unusual seriousness. Then he let out a long, low whistle.

"Oof. Yeah, we landed in a bad neighborhood, bud. This ain't just any town—this is a pit of soul-sucking, energy-draining joy-leeches. Real nasty types. I dated an Other once. She told me I had no sense of humor. And she said that my seams were loose. Can you imagine? I am very concerned about bag-hygiene."

Reggie swallowed. "Great. How do we beat them?"

Felix smirked. "Beat them? Oh no, kid, there's no beating them. They are professional Others. They have no conscience or empathy toward anyone. You can't win."

"Then what do we do?"

Felix's stitched mouth curved into a mischievous grin. "How many diamonds we got?"

Reggie blinked. "That's right, the frog. I think I still have one purchase left."

Jinx, the ever-annoying magic frog, croaked loudly from nowhere, appearing on a rooftop, arms crossed like he'd been expecting them. Though it was far too large for him, he still carried his dark leather bag filled with items to purchase.

"Oh? Finally remembered I exist? Fine. One purchase. Choose wisely, boy." He jumped to a stump beside Reggie.

Felix peered into Jinx's leather frog-bag, his grin widening. Unfortunately, he took that moment to hit on the sweet, dark leather number. "Hey, baby, what ya' doing hanging out with a slimy reptile like this one, eh? I like your stitches. What d'you say after this level is over, we get some downtime, maybe even a rub with some romantic leather oil? Hmmm? What's the matter, frog got your tongue?"

He turned to Reggie, "Too bad. She's a looker but doesn't say much."

"It's amphibian, not reptile, you lunatic," huffed the frog. "And leave my bag alone, you lecherous pouch."

"Maybe she doesn't speak English. Let me try something. Sprechen Sie polyester?" No answer.

"Are you just stupid?" Jinx said to Felix.

"I'll have you know that I have a very high thread count, Kermit," said Felix, as he inspected the inside of the leather bag. "My father was a well-used fieldwork bag involved in some serious ethnographic research. Before modeling for Dior, my mother was an international diplomatic pouch. I was born with some first-class weave DNA."

"Ooooh, now here's something interesting!" said Felix

enthusiastically. "Is that the Cognitive Behavioral Therapy 5000? Haven't seen one since therapy—I mean, not therapy for me, mind you. No... uh... it was for a friend, you know. I'm good."

"Felix, what are you doing?!" Reggie barked urgently.

"Relax, kid. I've got this. Hey, slimeball, we'll take the CBT 5000 for five diamonds."

Jinx reluctantly tossed the CBT 5000 to Reggie. "Enjoy, kid. Good luck not losing your mind. Only three diamonds left."

Reggie turned the object over in his hands. A mirror. A simple wooden-handled mirror with "CBT 5000" carved along the edge.

"What in the world do we need with a mirror?"

Felix's grin stretched. "Hold it up. Look at the Others through it."

Reggie frowned but obeyed. The moment he raised the mirror, the world shifted. The Others—the sneering, jeering, hateful villagers—changed. Through the mirror, he didn't see cruel faces. He saw broken ones. Every single one of them was hunched, pale, weak. Their eyes weren't sharp with mockery; they were dull with exhaustion, loneliness and fear of discovery.

The man who had spat at him? His reflection showed deep, sunken eyes, like those of someone who had cried too long but had forgotten why. The woman who insulted his hair? In the mirror, she was curled into herself, like she had never felt safe. The child who mocked him? Shivering. Arms wrapped tightly around herself, desperately looking for her mommy.

They weren't strong. They were scared. They weren't laughing at him. They were laughing to survive. Felix's voice was quieter now, unusually soft.

"They don't tear you down because they hate you, kid," said an unfamiliar voice.

"Wait, who said that?" Reggie looked around the crowded street.

"Hello, I am Carol, the Cognitive Behavioral Therapy 5000. Greetings! You asked for my help, apparently."

Reggie inspected the mirror once more until he was assured that he wasn't going nuts.

"So, like I said," Carol went on. "They do it because they hate a very deep part of themselves. It's all they know. We cognitive behavioral therapists refer to this as projection. It is a widespread psychological defense mechanism where a person criticizes others for traits they find distasteful, repugnant, or worthy of punishment *in themselves*. In reality, their subconscious brain is condemning themselves for the very same things. Irony, am I right? How bad is their own self-hatred? You can feel it in the nasty, nonempathetic and condemning way they treat others. In one sense, they are afraid that you will see their true selves and despise them."

Reggie's grip on the mirror tightened. His chest felt heavy. "You mean, they hate themselves?"

"Yes, of course, they don't even know you, and yet it appears like they do," added the mirror.

Reggie moved the mirror away and looked straight at the crowd. Yep, the Others still looked cruel. But through the mirror, they were just small and scared.

"By the way," added Carol, without much emotion, just matter-of-fact, "most bullying stems from much the same thing. Good to know, right?"

"So, what do I do?" Reggie whispered.

Felix's voice softened. "We walk away, dude. We don't fight. We don't argue. We just leave."

The mirror chirped in once more. "Yes, but don't expect that Others will let you leave with no reaction. They may even become a dangerous mob. Did I mention that most mob mentality is also a projection? Anyway, it is important when confronted with an Other, to remember the words of someone in your life who you are totally convinced adores you as you are. Someone who has always had your back and never treated you like an Other. Find your identity in their gaze, not the sad, disassembled emotional reactions of the Others. Another mirror once said that every one of us needs an 'other' who adores us like that, as we are. These poor Others haven't experienced that much, sad to say."

Reggie inhaled slowly. A few days ago, he would have said that about the King. Not now. Instead, he thought of his late mother. She was never disappointed in Reggie. She was his biggest fan. She once said that she would buy stock in Reggie. Oh, how he misses her.

For the first time in a few days, the weight began to lift.

When he felt emotionally prepared, he turned his back on the Others. As predicted, they erupted in a rage, hurling more insults, sneers, taunts and even a few still-warm cow-patties.

But their words didn't stick. Because now Reggie saw them for what they were. And he remembered who he was in his mother's eyes. He let them go.

The gray world cracked. Light poured in from the edges. Level Five was over.

Felix grinned. "Told ya. Easy-peasy."

Reggie let out a breath he hadn't realized he was holding.

As the world melted into the next level, he stuffed the CBT 5000 into Felix's woolen mouth.

Something told him, he would need her again.

IO

LEVEL SIX- THE PSYCHOBEAST

Reggie and Felix blinked awake, finding themselves perched on a high cliff before a ramshackle wooden fort. It wasn't so much a fort as it was a derelict cabin with long-forgotten delusions of grandeur, standing stark and lonely against the vast, empty sky. The oddity of its placement—high on a desolate ridge—struck them. What was it meant to protect, and where were its builders? The unsettling silence was broken only by the pounding wind, which howled through the many gaps in the fort's weathered timber.

Before the open gate, a grotesque collection of statues stood, each one frozen in a nightmarish pose: a woman fleeing in terror, a man contorted in a grimace of death, and a young boy crying out in frozen anguish. The tableau felt wrong, like a macabre welcome rather than a peaceful entry.

"Frog!" Reggie yelled, breaking the silence. "What is all of this?"

"Greetings, questers," Jinx replied, his voice dripping with amusement. This time, he wore yellow designer sunglasses that were far too big for his green head. "Welcome to Level 6. We are still trying to come up with a glitzy title. Maybe Stone-Cold Killer? Or This is the End. But for now, we are going with The Attack of the Psychobeast. You need no new identity. You can just be yourself—not that it will help you much. No one has ever managed to pass this level. You will see why in..." the frog said, glancing at the tiny timepiece on his even tinier green wrist, "oh, maybe an hour or three."

Reggie's frustration was palpable. "What is all this, you toad?"

Felix shivered, his voice betraying his growing unease. "Yeah, what's with all the creepy statues?"

"Ah, so many questions, so few answers," Jinx said with a dark chuckle. "By the way, for future reference—that is, if you have a future—the word frog comes from the Old English word frosc, which had variants such as frox and forsc. Frogs have smooth, somewhat slimy skin. Toads have dry, warty skin. Frogs have long legs, built for jumping—see? Toads have shorter legs and prefer to get around by crawling. As you can see, I am a very handsome frog, if I do say so myself."

"You know that the French eat frog legs, right?" Felix blurted out. "Cooked in butter and garlic. Yummy."

"How utterly distasteful of you to bring up that horrific, genocidal practice," said Jinx defensively. "Hmmm, so, where was I? First, good news! You've earned 10 more diamonds, bringing your total to 13. The store is open, though I doubt anything in my inventory will be of much use."

"What do you mean by that you croaker?" Reggie frowned, his patience thinning.

Jinx flashed a predatory grin. "Why don't you take a look behind you, beyond the fortification?"

They turned and saw in the distance the unmistakable silhouette of the King's castle loomed against the horizon.

"Hey, isn't that the King's castle?" Felix exclaimed.

"Indeed it is," Jinx confirmed. "Remarkable, isn't it? This trial is practically in his backyard. And yet, you're entirely on your own—once again."

"Maybe we'll pop over and say hello when we're done here," Reggie mused, half-joking.

Jinx's dry, rattling laugh filled the air. "Hmmm, I'm afraid that's wishful thinking."

"Oh yeah? We pouches have a saying..."

"Here we go again," muttered Reggie.

"Oh, you unfortunate uninitiate!" continued Felix. "Be optimistic. Optimistically assume things will go horribly wrong in new and interesting ways."

"Jinx, ignore him. What are you talking about?" Reggie demanded, growing impatient.

Jinx's smile widened, showing his teeth. "You stand on the mountain of a psychopathic killing machine. This is not some Other spouting unfortunate, perhaps, well-deserved criticisms. The Psychobeast has slaughtered countless victims—warriors, women, children, even their pets. I have heard she particularly dislikes snarky man-bags."

Jinx turned his body toward Felix, hanging at Reggie's belt.

"Hmmf!" responded Felix.

"No one," continued Jinx, holding the huge sunglasses in one of his tiny, webbed hands, "who has set foot on this ridge has lived to tell the tale. No one."

A heavy silence fell, and the wind seemed to echo the warning.

"So," Felix spoke slowly, trying to regain his composure,

"we can't... stay inside the fort? Lock the door and wait it out?"

Jinx's low chuckle was tinged with something darker. "If you think a few rotten planks will protect you, be my guest. But don't say I didn't warn you. Just look for yourself. The walls are not up to the task. Arrows, bolts, or swords won't save you either. You can't run. The only way out is 200 feet down to the sharp granite rocks below. You're trapped."

The tension was magnified, the idyllic scenery now tainted by an overwhelming sense of dread. Reggie and Felix exchanged a grim look, silently asking themselves what kind of beast could create such terror—and, more importantly, how they would possibly survive it.

"The beast is coming," Jinx continued ominously. "Like I said, it could be minutes or hours, but once she realizes someone has entered her territory, she will not hesitate. Oh dear, I realized—this is probably a perfect time for a smarter-than-average frog with both legs to skedaddle. Just remember, you can always use the Go to Trial card. You may want to have it ready."

"Wait," Reggie said, his eyes narrowing. "What's in your bag that we can use?"

Jinx waved his tiny frog hand dismissively, pulling items from the seemingly infinite depths of his satchel. "A coil of rope, a hammer, a magic wand—though no one knows what it does—and some soap. But now's not the time for personal hygiene. Oh, and no, I do not see any more wildcards—too bad."

Reggie quickly assessed the situation. "I'll take the rope."

"Hmmm, an interesting choice as usual," Jinx said with a smirk, vanishing before Reggie could ask any more questions.

Felix was quiet. Too quiet. Reggie noticed his unease and turned to his companion. "Felix, you okay?"

"Hey buddy, those statues… they're not statues," Felix finally murmured.

Reggie felt a chill creep down his spine. "What do you mean?"

"They're petrified people," Felix replied, his voice barely above a whisper.

Reggie cursed under his breath. "That's not good news."

Felix nodded and said with a sarcastic bite, "Yeah, no kidding. But good thing we have rope."

Reggie laughed nervously. "Yeah, I probably should've taken the soap. Then at least we would be clean when we die." They both laughed, but it hardly diminished the seriousness of their situation.

Felix shot him a look. "What kind of monster can do that to people? Something that's not afraid of arrows or swords."

Reggie circled the fort, examining it. "It's not much—a 20-foot square of logs, 15 feet high—constructed poorly, hastily, and plastered together with dung. Its back is right up against the cliff edge."

Felix's voice broke through his thoughts. "You thinking what I'm thinking?"

"Paremanja," Reggie said with a confident nod, the plan forming in his mind.

"Yep, that's the one," agreed Felix.

Reggie groaned. "Sure, but we'd need a whole team, with tools and levers…"

"Oh, did I forget to mention?" Felix said knowingly. "The Drukyl dragons gave me something for you. You know, if I ever saw you again."

Felix cleared his throat with a deliberate rasp, paused to

let the sound hang in the air. Then in one smooth motion, he spat a small whistle onto the ground. Reggie recognized it immediately. It was very similar to the one Rahgornah had given him, the dragon storyteller. "If you ever need help, blow this and we will come immediately."

Reggie always wore the whistle around his neck, at least until Dolos removed it along with everything else when this horrid game began.

"We've got to move fast." Reggie's hand trembled as he reached for the thin silver whistle. He put it to his lips and blew with all his might. A high-pitched, sharp sound echoed over the ridge.

It only took a minute or two for the great Drukyl dragon Rahgornah to appear overhead, his massive wings beating the air with an intimidating whoosh.

[Storyteller's Note: If you have read "The Tale of the Orphan Magician," you will be familiar with Rahgornah. He was the actual storyteller and a stepbrother of Reggie during his time with the Drukyl dragons.]

"Greetings, my stepbrother! I've been worried about you," the dragon said, his voice a booming rumble. "What is all of this?" he said, looking over at the small fort and statues.

"Later, I can't take the time to explain now, we only have an hour or so. I wish I could. But I do want to thank you for your help with the pirate ship. I assume that was you?"

Rahgornah's cheeks turned red from embarrassment. "I am glad that I could be of service, my brother."

"Hey, wait a minute," announced Felix. We may have

overlooked the obvious Plan B. Why don't we just hitch a ride on Rahgornah and fly out of here?"

"No," said Reggie. "I thought about that too. But I am not sure what magic Dolos is using. I am pretty sure we would be brought right back. We must complete the levels. Somehow we are going to have to defeat this beast, whatever she might be."

"Okay, Peremanja it is." If a pouch could shrug, that is what Felix would have done.

"Rahgornah, I need another huge favor," said Reggie, smiling. "I need you to fly to Qayeen and bring back as many of the Street Shadows as you can, with their tools. I don't know how much time we have. So ASAP."

"Consider it done," Rahgornah said, and was skyborne the very next moment. Within 15 minutes, over a dozen Street Shadows arrived, their tools at the ready. After quick high fives and hugs, Reggie, Felix, and the Shadows quickly began dismantling the fort, making necessary adjustments to trap the mysterious, murderous beast, whoever or whatever it—or she—might look like.

One of the youngest Shadows was instructed to keep an eye out for anything coming from the woods or from the sky that surrounded the ridge.

The work was grueling, but with everyone's help, they made it happen. When Rahgornah had finally taken all the Shadows away, Reggie leaned back on the gate and declared, "Done! I wish the ESS were here."

[Storyteller's Note: The Eagle Secret Service was the King's special forces, made up of experienced fighters from all species who were skilled in the art of fighting overwhelming

enemies. Reggie and Felix had linked up with them to stop a
war that had engulfed the entire continent of Amaratzim. You
can read about it in The Tale of the Orphan Magician.]

Just then, a blood-curdling scream echoed from the dark
shadows of the forest.

Felix swallowed. "Contact! Time to go kinetic."

They rushed into the fort, slamming the gate shut just as a
huge, morbidly obese, hulking figure emerged from the dark
shadows of the forest. It was a Medusa gorgon, more
terrifying than either of them could have ever imagined. It
was a female version of Dolos. No, that's not fair to Dolos.
This was an angry, rabid, feral, undocile, beastly, or, as the
Germans say, ungezähmt manifestation of the head gorgon.
She was 17 feet tall, covered in green scales, and her eyes
glowed with a sickly yellow light. Her monstrous form was a
grotesque mix of marble and rotting flesh, and her hissing
snakes seemed to move as though alive, hungry and furious.
Think of it this way: if Ursula, the sea witch, hooked up with
Sigourney Weaver's Alien and had an offspring—our two
heroes saw her.

Reggie gritted his teeth. "Don't look at her face."

Felix's voice shook. "You look away. I don't even have
eyes."

[Storyteller's Note: A bit of history, if you please. Long ago—
far from Amaratzim—there slithered a monstrous gorgon
named Medusa. Forget braids, waves, or even dreads, her
hair game was nothing but venomous, snapping serpents. She
was the very definition of "a bad hair day." Worse still, she

delighted in turning the curious to stone with a single glance.
Moral of the tale? Never meet a gorgon's eyes with your own.
In fact, should you spot a psychotic, growling snake-woman
writhing your way—don't argue, don't negotiate—just run.]

The Medusa stormed forward, her claws slashing at the fort's fragile walls. Reggie was quick, pushing a sharpened stake through a gap to strike her—but it only made her laugh, a horrible sound that reverberated in the air.

"You think you can hide?" she bellowed, her deep feral voice shaking the earth. She was an avalanche of fury; every breath she took was vibrating with rage and pain. The snakes atop her head hissed and snapped, their fangs dripping venom as if they shared in her eternal bitterness.

"This pile of sticks won't save you."

The fort groaned as she tore through it. It was clear that it wouldn't hold much longer. Reggie's heart raced. He knew it was only a matter of time before the Medusa would destroy everything in her path.

"Hold steady!" Reggie shouted, bracing himself. He swung the rope under his arms, tightening it against the crossbar at the back of the fort. "Don't look!"

Felix's voice crackled. "Is it time?"

"Not yet," Reggie whispered. "Not yet."

Then, with a deafening explosion, the door of the fort shattered into a cloud of dust and debris. And there she stood, the Medusa. Her monstrous form loomed only 15 feet in front of Reggie. The ground shook as she let out a loud, feral growl —a sound so hideous, so totally nonhuman, it seemed to come straight from the depths of nightmares.

In an instant, she charged at him with terrifying speed.

Lowering her head like a vicious bull, she aimed her horns directly at his chest.

"Oscar Mike, on the move now?" said Felix sarcastically.

Reggie barely had time to jump in the air, all his weight supported by the rope. The Medusa was surprised that Reggie had escaped her lunge, but it didn't matter. In two terrifying steps, she realized the truth too late. There was no floor, only a gaping hole. Her monstrous form careened down the steep, jagged slope, her final scream echoed as she plummeted toward the sharp granite rocks below.

[Storyteller's Note: Now, here's where I should let you in on the secret of Paremanja—the trap Reggie and Felix had perfected in Amaratzim, in a northern mining town where a massive grizzly had been terrorizing the locals. The beast was unstoppable. Traps didn't work; crossbow bolts dipped in sedatives barely slowed it down. Nothing.

In desperation, Felix devised a plan—one that seemed so crazy it might work. They built a rickety hut near the forest where the bear had been spotted, and Reggie sat outside, deliberately making noise and irritating the beast. The idea was simple: get the bear so enraged that it wouldn't even notice the trap. Sure enough, the bear charged, furious at the bait. Reggie, running like mad, dashed into the hut, leaving the door wide open. The bear followed without hesitation, but a few steps in, the beast fell into a 30-foot opening, landing hard at the bottom. Reggie had constructed a house with no floor directly over a deadly hole.]

. . .

The whole thing worked in Paremanja, against all odds. However, with the Medusa, they had to tweak the plan. With the help of the Street Shadows, they dismantled the fort and rebuilt it with the back hanging far over the cliff edge, supported only by reinforced stakes at the front of the fort. If the Medusa had been in her right mind, maybe she could have seen the trap, but she was too enraged to notice. When she charged at Reggie, not looking down, it was all over. She fell straight into the crevasse below, disappearing from sight.

In magician terms, Reggie was that shiny little object that misdirects the viewer's sight, so they don't see the trick happening somewhere else. "I can't believe that worked," chuckled Felix. "The plan had a 2% success rate. Which is 1.5% higher than usual."

"Funny, dude!" replied Reggie. "I am just as surprised as you."

Felix added, "Did you see the look on her face?"

"Excuse me?" Reggie raised an eyebrow, still gripping the rope. "Do I look like a statue?"

Felix grinned. "Hmm, I plead the fifth, because what I might say would definitely incriminate me. I will take this opportunity to share a wise saying passed down from elder man-bags in times past. The plan shouldn't have worked. But neither should dragons fly, or Brussels sprouts taste good, or, frankly, everything about your haircut."

As they caught their breath, a voice echoed from below—one that sent a chill down their spines.

"Please… help me," came the broken cry of the Medusa. Her fall had been halted by a single tree that stuck out from the side of the cliff. She was barely hanging on for life.

Felix stared in shock. "Are you kidding me? Now she needs help?"

Reggie hesitated, eyes darting between the crevasse and Felix. "It's a trick. It must be."

But then the sobs began. The Medusa—or rather Euryale, as they would soon learn—seemed desperate, and something about it felt real.

Reggie swung back to safety, gripping the rope. "Give me the CBT 5000."

Felix looked at him, confused. "What are you planning?"

"I don't know, but I think I can look at her without turning to stone if I use the mirror."

Felix wasn't convinced. "Yeah, but why would you want to see her face?"

Reggie shook his head. "I'm not sure, but I have to try."

With a steady hand, Reggie held the mirror up to the edge of the crevasse. As his eyes met the reflection, the truth hit him like a punch to the gut. It was very much like his experience looking at the Others.

Through the mirror's reflection, the vicious medusa beast wasn't a monster at all, not really. The face staring back at him was full of pain, weariness and something far deeper than rage. It was a girl—well, a female of some kind anyway—trapped in a cursed existence she likely never asked for. Her eyes were hollow, the glow of her ill-fated identity flickering like a dying flame.

And there, etched into her very being, was Dolos. His presence, his cruelty, was all over her: his anger, his need for control, his refusal to love. She was a victim—an unfortunate victim of Dolos—just like so many others.

"Hey, buddy. I think that she is Dolos' daughter!" exclaimed Reggie.

"I guess he just lost my vote for Father of the Year award!" quipped Felix.

Reggie's heart twisted. He knew what it was like to feel lost, to wonder if anyone cared. But this... this was different. Euryale had been born into a nightmare, one manipulated and used by Dolos himself. She had spent her life fighting for a father who would never love her, living in the shadow of lies and cruelty. No wonder she was angry. No wonder she wanted to destroy everything.

"Her name is Euryale," Reggie shouted down into the abyss, his voice filled with sympathy. "And I'm not about to sit here and let her drop to her death."

Felix muttered. "But how the heck do we get her out?"

Reggie paused, then grinned. "I've got an idea. Hand me the whistle again."

Felix eyed him warily. "Oh no. You're not gonna..."

"Yep," Reggie cut him off, already blowing the high-pitched whistle. Within moments, the mighty wings of Rahgornah beat the air above them once more.

Rahgornah landed gracefully, his massive form dwarfing the two. "What's going on, Reggie?"

"Can you help us?" Reggie explained the situation, detailing how Euryale was not merely a monster but a victim of Dolos' cruelty. "I think I saw the real her through the mirror. I think she needs help, but I can't do it alone."

Rahgornah looked thoughtful. "Are you sure? She's quite dangerous."

Reggie nodded. "I'm not sure about anything, but I need to try."

With careful precision, Rahgornah lowered a rope to Euryale. "Tie this around you. When you're ready, give it a tug."

Minutes later, and with a great deal of dragon sweat and straining, Rahgornah lifted Euryale up and back to the mountain peak, her form awkwardly suspended by the rope. The dragon was careful to avoid looking at her face. Reggie, too, kept his eyes on the mirror, never daring to look at her directly.

Once Euryale realized she was safe, her towering form seemed to fold in on itself as she sank to her knees with a trembling exhale. Even the snakes that enveloped her head seemed to be calmer and at ease. Relief coursed through her, and, for a moment, Reggie wasn't sure if she was physically spent or simply overwhelmed.

When she looked up at Reggie, her tear-filled, yellow, bulbous eyes shone with a gratitude more profound than any words could convey. Her voice, low and still unsteady, finally broke the silence. "That... that was the kindest thing anyone has ever done for me. I don't know what to say. How did you know I wouldn't kill you just to make my father happy with me?"

"I didn't. I saw something through the mirror. I lost my father, you know? It's not the same, but we are both kinda orphans." Reggie didn't know what else to say, but he carefully put his hand on her slumped shoulder—with the snakes' permission, of course.

"Look, uh... Miss Euryale, I'm a street magician, not a counselor. I am beginning to see that I need one. But it seems to me that it might be wise to get away from your father, Dolos. He'll only hurt you more."

Euryale nodded slowly, still trying to wrap her head around an act of kindness—far too rare in her life. "I know. But where would I go? Who would want this?" she said with deep disgust, waving her hand up and down her huge feral body.

"Look, I can't volunteer anyone, but I am pretty sure that I know someone who would be willing to speak with you. You know, like a counselor," said Reggie, thinking of course of Noomai. "I could give her this mirror. Who knows? Maybe she can help."

"I appreciate the thought. Maybe, if you survive what my father has in store for you next... well, let's meet here again. I'm not going anywhere. My father has me held hostage here."

"If I know Noomai, she can help with that, too. I have seen what she can do with your father."

"So," said Euryale, as she looked around to see if anyone might be listening, "maybe I can pay you back a little. You've endured trials of ice, fire and water. You weren't supposed to survive. But you did. All that is left is wind—but not just any wind. Don't let your guard down. That's all I know. I can help you no more. And I don't know specifics, but the King is not going to help you."

"How do you know that?"

"I just do... Look, I've stuck my neck out for you. I can't say anymore. You are on your own. And don't trust my father."

She turned. Her massive, sad form disappeared into the woods.

As Reggie watched her go, a heavy silence hung in the air. The world had shifted, what had begun as a battle for survival had turned into something far more complicated.

Then he turned to look at the distant castle. He finally knew for sure that the King was not coming to his aid. Even after all of this, he had hoped beyond hope that the King would change his mind at last—maybe see how valuable a warrior he was, or a worthy son. But no.

Something happened inside him. Maybe we could call it

an inner hardness, a steeling of his energies to not merely survive but to conquer.

"We'll beat this thing, Fee. That'll show the King. He underestimated me. He will regret rejecting me. That's for sure."

As he was talking to himself, his world was disassembled into shadows and darkness once more. Level Seven was nigh.

What Reggie couldn't see—and of course, Dolos would never want him to see—were the tears rolling down the King's face as he quietly watched his faithful servant suffer in this most horrific trial.

II

LEVEL SEVEN: SPIRIT PEAKS

When Reggie opened his eyes, he found himself hanging precariously on a sheer vertical ice cliff, with a single frayed woven rope. Spirit Peaks stretched endlessly above, its jagged edges slicing through the storm-ridden sky. The wind roared like a wounded beast as he looked around at his precarious position. The narrow ledge was only sufficient for the toes of his boots.

Still no King. But by now, Reggie expected his absence.

Each moment on the frigid cliff felt like it was met with resistance—not from enemies, but from the sheer weight of existence itself.

"Don't let your guard down," Reggie remembered Euryale saying. But what did she mean?

The penetrating cold gnawed at his bones, the silence pressing against his brain like an unseen shadow force. It was not just a physical cold; it was also an emotional one.

"Whew, baby," Reggie yelled to Felix, trying to be heard over the wind. "It is doggone cold up here."

No response. "Hey, no fair, buddy. You are keeping warm in your little woolen home, aren't you?"

Still nothing. Reggie looked down. To his shock, Felix was gone. Had he fallen? Knocked off between the levels?

"Felix!" Reggie shouted, voice strained. "FELIX!"

Yelling in sub-zero temperatures is very dangerous. It can cause a rush of frigid air to fill one's lungs, causing significant damage, irritation to vulnerable airways, and symptoms like discomfort, coughing, and shortness of breath. That is precisely what happened. Reggie fell into a coughing fit that only exacerbated his situation.

Then, just inches from Reggie's face, a strange twelve-inch diameter window swirled open. Jinx appeared—or at least his head did—shielded from all the wind and cold, wearing little earmuffs and tiny gloves.

"Greetings, boy, or let me call you by your new avatar name, Polar Player. Welcome to Level 7: Spirit Peaks."

Reggie cut him off. "You slimy, little amphibian, what have you done with Felix? Where is he? I demand that you give him back, now!"

Jinx smirked. "First, I'd remind you, you are in no position to demand anything. Look around Polar. You're hanging by your toes on a W16-grade ice slope. I would spend my time figuring out how to climb."

"Second, we have become aware of a nasty little breach of the rules on the last level. It appears that you have received some assistance before. Bad boy! We can't allow that to keep happening. Imagine if the word got out—players cheating on the levels? We can't have that."

"Third, the Shadow Lord is quite upset about how you treated his daughter. She is inconsolable. He doesn't know what you did, but she can't even speak to him about it."

"Rather she won't, you dumb polliwog," Reggie snapped.

Jinx sniffed. "Hmmmf. Nevertheless. For those serious violations, we are taking away some privileges. First, look at your wrist. You no longer have any diamonds, so you can't purchase anything from the game store to help you. Second, we have removed your nasty little friend Felix from your belt. No more help from him—not that he was much help before, to be honest. So, any questions, street rat?"

Reggie had to shout over the loud, rushing winds. "What am I supposed to do here?"

"Why, reach the top, of course—this time, totally on your own. Nobody is coming for you. Only 3,500 feet to go."

"But relax. As I have said before, we're not without a sense of fairness. The sun's coming up soon, it should warm up to a cozy minus 35° F. Still, we gave you some warm clothes, a hooded woolen robe with a fur collar. There are mono-point crampons on your boots and climbing hooks and screws on your belt. You're also armed with a longsword and a silver dagger. You never know. Maybe that will give you some encouragement. Oh—and a candle."

Reggie frowned. "But it's unlit? Can I have some matches?"

"Oh," Jinx chuckled rudely, totally insensitive to Reggie's situation. "They wouldn't do you any good in this wind anyway. It is a trial after all. I will say it again: there's always a Plan B."

Then the swirling window snapped shut.

Reggie was isolated and alone.

No Felix.

Still no King.

A brutal gust of bitterly cold wind knocked him off his perch, leaving him helplessly swinging in the air, buffeted back and forth by quickly shifting blasts. He felt like he was in a prizefight against an overwhelming foe. Each time he found another ledge—even the narrowest toe hold—another squall ripped him away.

The sword fell from his belt first, clanging violently against the ragged rocks below. A large rock struck his left shoulder, missing his skull by only inches. He was sure his shoulder was dislocated. Reggie wondered if it wasn't a coincidence. He scanned the slope above him but saw only fog and snow.

He twisted his body, desperate for another foothold, but only found a tiny ledge for a single foot. His situation was becoming increasingly dire. Moving, frightening shadows flickered at the edges of his vision—whispers curled around them like smoke—bony fingers reached out toward his face.

"You have failed this time," a heavy voice murmured. "You cannot climb this mountain," it growled.

A specter appeared, drifting on the howling wind, a twisted echo of some actual or former being. Its deathly contorted face was half-formed, frozen in an expression of sorrow—maybe? Shame? Anger? Reggie couldn't tell.

It reached out its murky arms and grabbed Reggie by his throat, strangling him. Reggie hesitated briefly, then athletically twisted out of the spirit's grasp, pushing off his icy hold as far away as he could.

An overwhelming exhaustion threatened to consume him. Each doubt, each fear, manifested as an unbearable weight, emotionally dragging him down. He was lost and alone. The orphan magician was back to where he started, an angry teen, blaming the world for his bad hand—well, that's not totally true. He blamed only one person—the King.

The inhabited, malignant gale screamed through the crags

—every blast like another hand trying to rip him from the mountain, over and over. His breaths became dangerously shallow and oxygen-deprived. His fingers were intolerably stiff and barely able to grasp the climbing hooks.

Whispered voices ceaselessly pounded Reggie's ears from all directions. "The King never cared," one female specter snarled, with a hollow, inhuman voice. "What were you thinking? You were alone when you were found, and you always will be. It's you."

The vile thoughts curled around Reggie's mind like creeping, strangling frost. His faith had carried him through countless trials. Still, here, in the bitter solitude of Spirit Peaks, there was only doubt, a piercing paranoid-driven depression. He knew he wouldn't make it much farther.

Still, the proud Reggie, no stranger to being alone and isolated, gritted his teeth, forcing himself onward. With every agonizing move, his resolve continued to unravel. At one point, he even saw himself falling—like it was a dream, but far too real—his helpless body tumbling endlessly into the cold abyss, the wind swallowing his final scream. In his vision, he saw himself kneeling before the Shadow Lord, surrendering at last. Then, he saw himself pulling the *Go to Trial* card from his pouch, demanding the King answer for his silence.

That temptation gnawed at him, raising the obvious, reasonable questions. "Why not now? Why not here?" Reggie couldn't tell if he was yelling the words or if it just felt that way in his brain.

"This King doesn't deserve to be protected by me," he heard his voice bellow. But was it his? He couldn't tell anymore. "His Royal Highness has proven to be a real disappointment and deserves to be taken to trial—the more

public, the better. If I don't do it, who will? If not now, when?
I want to shove all of this in his royal pompous face," said the
familiar voice. Maybe his, maybe not.

A deep ache settled in his chest. His hands trembled as he
reached into his pouch, his fingers brushing against the card's
now-worn edges. The King had asked for trust. But trust in
what? The emptiness? The abandonment? The betrayal? The
isolation? The silence? The rejection? The capriciousness?

Another powerful gust of wind belted Reggie once again,
causing him to swing far away from the cliff. But then gravity
drove him crashing back into it with all his weight. He heard a
loud crack and felt an intense pain in his chest. Maybe a
broken rib, or maybe worse. There was no way he was
climbing 50 feet, much less 3,500 feet. It was over.

The cacophony of shrill, unearthly cries attacked him with
increasing velocity: "You are not strong enough. You will fail.
You will perish out here, and no one will care. No one will
even know. You are a loser, boy."

The specters multiplied. "Do it!" said a smoky rendition
of that mangy cur Belyadad, with his patented southern drawl.
"Do it," cried the writhing elephant, Uphaz, followed by the
same shriek from the Magpie, Sippor. Worse were the ghostly
images of his mom and dad bellowing, "Do it, son! Do it!"
Then the coup de grâce: It was Felix himself who appeared,
surging toward him, threatening to knock him off the ledge.
"Buddy, what's up? Just do it."

Though part of Reggie's brain told him these wraiths were
not real, another part of him grasped hold of them with all his
being. Reggie clenched his jaw. What *was* he doing? Why *was*
he hesitant? Why did he feel the need to defend the King's
reputation? After all, the King wasn't defending him, was he?
All he wanted were answers.

He shut his freezing eyes and imagined himself standing in front of the throne. "Tell me, my King, why did you abandon me? Why did you let Dolos do this to me? I have done nothing wrong. I have been honest and faithful. You know that. I just want an explanation. I just want public vindication. I want an apology from you. I want you to admit you were wrong, and I was right. I want to go to trial, you disappointing King."

An explosion of light erupted from above. Over the sound of the crushing wind and the increasing volume of whispers and accusations, laughter roared from a single individual.

Dolos had won.

12

THE TRIAL OF THE KING

Reggie opened his eyes and found himself in a warm, sterile courtroom filled with the elite of the great kingdom. Lords, knights, and other officials quietly stared from the rows of seats. At the front stood a towering dais, adorned with a large set of Scales of Justice and the King's royal seal etched into the wood. Everything about this place radiated power and authority—Reggie felt torn. In one sense, he wondered if he should be here. But in another, he was finally going to get his questions answered—maybe.

"Okay, okay," said a nervous elf, awkwardly seated to Reggie's right. He was going through a manila folder of documents. "Highly irregular. Truly a very dangerous gambit, young man. Are you sure you want to proceed? You are taking the Great King to trial."

"Wait, tell me who you are?" Reggie asked, blinking in confusion.

"I am Ilyahoo," the elf replied. "The *H* is silent."

Reggie stared at him, trying to process that. *"A silent H?"* he thought. *"This is not beginning well."*

"Call me Ilya," the elf continued. "Everyone else does. I am your court-appointed prosecutor."

Ilyahoo was every bit the refined elf. Dressed in a dark green robe trimmed with gold, his long platinum hair was braided neatly, and gold-rimmed spectacles perched on his sharp nose. His voice, calm yet firm, carried a melodic elven lilt that belied his razor-sharp legal mind. Though relatively young by elven standards at 208, he was an expert in kingdom legal precedent and obscure laws and had a reputation for incisive questioning.

"I must say, I'm more used to prosecuting pickpockets and thieves. There is little precedent for this. I've been in the King's Attorney's Office for 160 years and have never seen— nor heard of—such a foolish endeavor. I mean, what exactly is the charge?"

"Wait, wait." Reggie held up both hands. "I didn't *want* to do this, but I didn't have any choice."

"Lad, we always have a choice."

"No, that's not what I meant. Can we go somewhere and talk, like... privately?"

"Yes, of course," Ilya said, rising from his seat. "We have a little time before the judge arrives. There's a room we can use. Follow me."

As they left the courtroom, Reggie felt his stomach drop. He spotted familiar faces—Nomos, Noomai, Rahgornah and so many others he counted as friends. I, Jeremy, was there, sitting nervously in the third row. "They're all here to witness this?" Reggie thought, dismayed. "Maybe this wasn't such a good idea after all."

He wanted answers and vindication. Who wouldn't?

Once inside a small conference room, Ilya shut the door.

Reggie sank into a chair at the table, now feeling foolish and vulnerable.

"Okay, young man," Ilya said, folding his hands. "Tell me what's really going on."

Reggie cleared his throat. "Look, I was minding my own business in Qayeen with my crew, the Street Shadows..."

"Yes, I see it in your file," Ilya interjected. "You started a gathering for street kids called the Street Shadows, giving them a safe place to live, work, a sense of family and treatment for addiction. You have a construction division, a manufacturing warehouse, a food distribution network, a special film area where you recycle Marvel sequels—very admirable and a great public service. I'm sure the King is grateful. And yet here we are, with you taking him to court."

Reggie shook his head. "No, that's not it. I woke up and found myself in an excruciating seven-level game called *Shadowbound* under the control of Dolos, and, by the way... totally against my will."

"The gorgon?" Ilya's face went pale. "The professed deadly enemy of the King and everything he stands for?"

"Yes, the same. Why do you ask?"

"Well, I assumed you knew. Your trial request named the judge."

"Oh no..." Reggie's eyes widened. "It's Dolos?"

Ilya nodded gravely. "The same."

Reggie let out a shaky breath. "Oh my... King help me."

"Please continue," said Ilya, shaking his head.

"So, I didn't do anything to deserve this treatment—this punishment. I could have died on any of those levels. I can't figure out why I was subjected to that. No one came to rescue me, no one from the castle, no sign of the King. Nothing. I received no help at all, except for my magic pouch, Felix, and the Drukyl dragons. If I had committed a crime—been a traitor or in collusion with Dolos—then, yes, I'd understand. But I haven't. In fact, it's only been a few months since the King knighted me."

"Yes, I was there," Ilya said, tapping his chin. "It was quite an event."

"So, if I understand this correctly, you're accusing the King of not having your back?"

"Well… yeah… but first, I want—no, I'm demanding— that the King tell me what I did or didn't do to deserve this. I'm being treated like a terrorist or a criminal. It's not fair. And if I *did* do something horrible, I'll confess and beg for mercy. But I don't know what I did, and no one from the castle is forthcoming. What have I done to deserve this?"

"A formal writ of discovery, then," Ilya said slowly. "Young man, that's a far cry from putting the King on trial."

"What choice did I have?" Reggie demanded. "I was kidnapped by Dolos, forced into a seven-level gauntlet against my will, all while some stupid frog named Jinx kept changing his hats and followed me around!"

"I see." The elf nodded sympathetically and wrote down frog with hats. "And how did you get here today?"

"At the beginning, they gave me this magic card," Reggie explained, sliding the card across the table. "It says, *Go to Trial.*"

"That's it?" Ilya frowned. "So, at some point, you played this card?" He made air quotes with his fingers.

"Yes, I suppose I did, only a moment ago," Reggie confirmed.

"Human, this is no game." His eyes furrowed with frustration. "Go on, please," the elf said, leaning forward now.

"So, I guess I'm formally requesting that the court require

the King to tell me what, if anything, I've done to deserve such unfair and unjust treatment at the hands of Dolos."

Ilya arched an eyebrow. "Yes, but I understand that Dolos would treat you poorly—he's a gorgon, after all. Vengeful and sadistic. But he's not on trial here. Is that accurate? Instead, you are charging the King for not intervening on your behalf. You see my issue here? You seem to be letting Dolos slide."

Reggie's eyes burned with frustration. "No, I want justice for Dolos' crimes too. But, in one sense, I get why he is doing this. Dolos wants revenge; I understand that motive. I embarrassed him badly in Qayeen. I don't understand why the King has abandoned me." His voice cracked with the weight of his words.

"We embarrassed him badly in Qayeen," said a voice at Reggie's belt.

"Felix! Welcome back, buddy. I missed you. Jinx told me that they took you away because we cheated."

"They are accusing us of bad behavior. That's rich. That's the pot calling the basket... uh... the kettle calling the... uh... oh, you know what I mean."

"Wait, what... who's that?" asked Ilya.

"Oh, may I introduce my best friend, the magic man-bag, Felix?"

"My *H* is silent, too," quipped Felix. It made Reggie smile for the first time today.

The lawyer looked at his watch and urgently returned the conversation back to the upcoming trial.

"But why didn't the King do anything?" pleaded Reggie. "Why didn't he come to my aid? He didn't even acknowledge that I needed help. That's worse than anything Dolos did. I trusted the King—I believed he valued me. But now..." He looked away. "I have questions about my relationship with the King."

"And you tried asking?" Ilya prompted.

"Yes. I cried out to the King several times. Jinx said an official request was sent too—but I kind of doubt that happened. I begged the King to explain what was happening, to tell me if there was some higher purpose to all this suffering. I could handle that. But I can't handle the silence, unless it means the King has turned his back on me. That's what I am afraid of."

"So, we want to compel the King to explain his inaction regarding your recent kidnapping and torment," the elf summarized.

"Yes, I suppose so—in legal language. Can we do that?"

"We can attempt it," Ilya replied. "But this is a court of law, not marriage counseling. We can motion for an explanation, but this court has no real jurisdiction to force the King to talk. And you have ignited something far more serious, with longer-term consequences."

"What do you mean?"

He looked down at the one-page court docket. "You have officially charged the King with untrustworthiness, unkinglike behavior, and criminal indifference toward a citizen in his realm. If he's found guilty—and that is likely Dolos's plan— the King will be shamed. Publicly humiliated. For you to be vindicated, according to your charge, the King must admit malfeasance related to you."

"I am so confused," Reggie said.

"Perhaps the King will not appear," said Ilya. "Especially not with Dolos as the judge—this court has no real authority over him. But, in the court of public opinion, if he doesn't appear to answer your charges, he'll be seen as guilty anyway. The result is the same. That must be Dolos' gambit all along. He is using you."

Ilya studied Reggie intently. "I think you've been played, boy."

"But Ilya with a silent *H*, what's going on? I want the King's favor back. I had it a few months ago at my knighting. What changed? What did I do?"

"Let's follow your logic," Ilya replied. "You were in the King's favor. Then you were wrongly and unjustly victimized by Dolos, so you conclude that the King no longer favors you. You think he doesn't care, or that he's aligned with Dolos somehow?"

"Well... yes," Reggie mumbled, looking at the ground and shrugging. "I suppose."

"And conversely," the elf continued, "if the King still favored you, he wouldn't have allowed Dolos to torment you in the first place?"

"That makes sense to me," Reggie said.

"Have you considered a third option?" Ilya asked. "What if—even now, while you endure all these unjust trials—the King still favors you?"

Reggie frowned. "How could that be?"

"There's a term for this line of thinking," Ilya explained. "It's not law, but human nature. We elves have a longer vision and don't succumb to it so easily. It's called the *Retribution Principle*."

From below the table came a small voice: "Helloooo," said Felix, sounding smug in an I-told-you-so manner.

"Yeah,' Reggie muttered. "I have a friend who told me about that. If I understand correctly, by doing the right things,

I expect to be treated well. But if I have done wrong, I shouldn't expect kindness. So, since I am being treated as a condemned criminal, I assumed that I'd done something wrong and this is what I deserve."

"Well stated," Ilya said. "Are you aware that the King is not bound by the *Retribution Principle* at a day-to-day level? In fact, one purpose of a King's so-be'd quest is to disabuse questers of that notion."

"So, you're suggesting I might be on a King's so-be'd quest?" Reggie asked.

"Nothing is more likely," Ilya said with a shrug. "You know this King is not what he appears. If it *is* an official royal quest—even though it might be a horribly distressing one, granted—there could be a reason the King doesn't intervene. It certainly does not imply implicitly or explicitly that you have done anything wrong, that you should be punished so, or that the King doesn't favor you anymore. If it is an official so be'd King's Quest; in the end, there will be glory in it for you. That should be very comforting."

He paused.

"Or it might not be a quest at all, and I am toast," shrugged Reggie.

"With a silent *H*," added Felix.

"But what possible reason could there be for not telling me what's going on?" Reggie demanded. "Isn't it my right to know?"

"Right?" Ilya raised an eyebrow. "You humans are always speaking of rights? Have you ever heard of any quester being told the full reason for their quest? Or any quester giving the King their permission? Seriously, boy, where have you been?"

Reggie opened his mouth to protest, but Ilya shook his

head. "We need to get back to the courtroom. We don't want
to make Judge Dolos wait, that will not go well for you."

Everything in the conference room froze. Ilya's mouth hung
open mid-word, and a hush settled over the air. Reggie
recognized the feeling. Time had been stopped once again, as
it had six times before.

Sure enough, Jinx hopped from a file cabinet behind
Reggie and landed on the conference table, gazing up with
huge brown eyes behind a hangman's head cover.

"Braaaap!" the frog croaked. "I was just kidding before.
This is your actual *Level Seven: The Trial of the King.* You are
assuming the role of plaintiff. But in reality, you are the King-
killer. I must say, you've made it much farther than any of us
thought you would. Lord Dolos is exceedingly pleased. Now,
it's time for someone to bring that foolish, capricious monarch
to trial in his own country. Today, if all goes according to
plan, you'll tear down his throne once and for all—and you
will be famous, lad."

"I don't want to be famous," Reggie spat. "I want to be
vindicated. I don't belong in this game—I did nothing to
deserve it." He paused, hearing the echo of his own words and
recalling the *Retribution Principle.*

"Croooak!" Jinx blinked. "Who said you did?"

Then Jinx disappeared just as quickly as he had appeared.

"It's time," said Ilya.

The courtroom doors creaked open, and an immediate hush fell over the room. All eyes turned to the judge, who entered with quiet authority, flanked by the court officers. "Now presiding," said the bailiff, "the Honorable High Judge Sir Dolos III." The audience groaned dismissively.

As the judge took his seat, everyone in the room—lawyers, witnesses, and the audience—awkwardly rose to their feet, a sign of respect for the court—certainly not for the judge.

Once the judge settled in, he nodded for everyone to be seated. The low murmur of the room faded into silence. The judge's voice rang out, clear and steady, as he called the case.

"The first trial on the docket, number 12654, Reginald Blackstone, aka Raziel the Magnificent, versus the so-called Great King of Garden City. The defendant is being charged with the high and shameful crimes of untrustworthiness, unkinglike behavior, and criminal indifference toward an honored citizen in his realm."

Dolos shook his head in disgust, making sure to milk his grand performance for all it was worth.

"What a tragedy that this kingdom has come to this, where we can't trust our leaders to have the backs of our respected, innocent citizens. Oh, how tragic it truly is." He grabbed a handkerchief from his robe pocket and dabbed his eyes to catch any tears.

"Who is here for the plaintiff?"

"Here, your honor. Ilyahoo—with a silent *H*—for the plaintiff."

"Who is here for the defendant?"

"Here, your honor. Noomai, the Royal Counselor for the defendant."

Reggie couldn't believe his ears. He had been too busy to

notice Noomai sitting at the defendant's bench. What had he done?

"Counselor Noomai," asked the judge insincerely. "Is the defendant expected to join us this morning?"

"With all due respect, your honor, take care. You are here at the grace of the defendant, but your leash is quite short. Don't make me come up there. You are the one who should be on trial for the way you have kidnapped and abused this poor boy."

"Allegedly kidnapped and abused the boy, I would remind you" barked the judge. "Counselor, I charge you with contempt of court. Your fine will be 500 guerrins. I warn you to hold your tongue. We are about the business of justice, fairness and right in this courtroom. I require appropriate decorum, if you please. So, be careful what side you find yourself on."

Noomai huffed and carefully sat down with the aid of her cane.

"Mr. prosecutor, are you ready with your statement?"

"I am, Judge." Ilyahoo's voice filled the massive room. He carefully and extensively outlined all the allegations reported by Reggie, maintaining a careful balance of clarity and gravity.

"We will present indisputable evidence along with witnesses that will prove beyond a shadow of a doubt that the King of Garden City has been unfaithful and indifferent toward a man whom he had knighted only weeks before. The only just outcome of this trial will be the King found guilty of unfaithfulness."

"Very well said, counselor. Madame Defendant, do you have a statement?"

"Not at this moment. I reserve the right to make my statement at a later time."

"Very well, Mr. Prosecutor. Call your first witness."

"The Prosecution calls the Great King of Garden City."

"This can't be good," said Felix. "You know, we man-bags have a saying for this: One moment it's bad. The next, you're arguing with a troll over snack rations."

13
FIRST WITNESS

For a moment, there was only silence. No one was sure if the King would come to the trial. That was the prosecutor's primary strategy, of course. If the King came, he would be forced to testify. If he did not come, that would be portrayed as an admission of guilt. Honestly, few expected him to honor this court and this judge by coming and possibly humiliating his reputation by subjecting himself to testimony.

The massive double doors in the back of the courtroom swung open with a thunderous boom, their gilded edges catching the candlelight as they revealed the figure beyond. A hush fell over the courtroom—then, a collective gasp.

The Great King stood at the threshold, draped in regal splendor. His cloak of deep crimson velvet cascaded behind him, embroidered with golden filigree that shimmered like fire. A jeweled crown rested upon his brow. His breastplate, polished to a mirror sheen, bore the sigil of his house—a tripart emblem of Right, Justice and Compassionate Presence.

. . .

[Storyteller's Note: For more information about the Royal Emblem, refer to "Tale of the Unlikely Prince." It would be well worth the research.]

"The Great King advanced forward, each footstep deliberate, his boots echoing against the marble floor like distant thunder. The scent of myrrh and aged leather clung to him, a presence both foreign and familiar. The courtroom, packed with nobles, scribes and commoners, seemed to shrink in his presence.

Whispers swirled among the onlookers, disbelief coloring every hushed word. He had come. He, the untouchable, the unreachable, had chosen to stand among them.

"Breathe!" Reggie thought, his pulse rate rising like a tsunami after a magnitude 8.6 earthquake. "In... out... in..."

With unwavering poise, the King strode down the central aisle, his gaze steady, unreadable. His expression gave away nothing—no anger, no sorrow, only an inscrutable certainty. The golden embroidery along his sleeves glowed in the flickering candlelight as he approached the witness chair.

And then, to the astonishment of all—he sat.

All held their breath. No king had ever taken this seat before. This was not a throne; it was not a place of rulership. It was a place of judgment, of questioning, of truth.

For the first time in history, the Great King had come to bear witness.

The judge quickly realized the King's gaze was fixed solely on him. The wager had come to this—to this moment. It was Dolos who smiled now. He knew what no one else knew: the King couldn't answer Reggie's questions. He could not explain why he hadn't intervened. He could not explain why he had remained silent. If he did, the wager would be forfeited and Dolos would win.

And yet, he was here. "Curious," thought Dolos. "What am I missing?"

After the King had taken his seat in the dock and sworn to tell the whole truth in his testimony, the prosecuting attorney rose carefully and addressed him.

"Your Highness, with all due respect—and I do mean that," said Ilyahoo with professionalism and more than appropriate deference. "It is my duty to do everything in my power to further my client's cause in this court today."

The King gave a slight nod. "I understand, Counselor. I encourage you to do your job faithfully and to the best of your ability. What questions would you ask of me? I am here because I want truth and justice to prevail."

He glanced toward the judge, his expression unreadable, yet tinged with something close to despair—if that were even possible in this venue.

Noomai smiled knowingly and cast a glance at Nomos in the first row. His eyes—wide as cake platters—betrayed his shock. He never expected the King to appear. And yet, there he was, in all his royal splendor. "This is bollocks," he muttered.

The prosecutor straightened his papers and cleared his throat. "Very well, Your Highness. You are aware that you stand accused of untrustworthiness, unkinglike behavior and criminal indifference toward a faithful, innocent citizen of your realm?"

"I am aware," the King replied evenly. Then, with a royal smirk, he added, "Are you aware that I have been accused of much worse?"

The audience burst into unexpected laughter.

The prosecutor smiled back. "Yes, I suppose so, Your Highness. But for now, please tell the court what defense you offer against these charges."

The King leaned forward. "I offer no defense."

A murmur rippled through the courtroom. The prosecutor hesitated. "Excuse me? You have come, I assume, because we subpoenaed you to answer these charges—charges brought forth by a man you knighted only days ago."

The King turned, his gaze locking onto Reggie. "I greet my faithful new knight, Sir Reggie." Then, he fixed his attention back on the courtroom. "No. The reason I am here is not to defend myself, but to ask Reggie a question or two."

A heavy silence settled over the room.

"Tell me, my valued faithful knight, where were you when humans and other species revolted against my throne in the Great Rebellion? Did you stand beside me and my son? Did you voice an opinion about the wall we were forced to raise around the Great Tree? Perhaps you had another idea?"

"Were you among the troops that defended Pirate's Cross decades ago? Did you lift even a single finger to help Berenice when her father abused her—when she was alone, afraid and had no one to turn to?"

"Did you offer me counsel during the Great Trollian War? Or during the vicious attack on the Mahtesian Islands, when violent warlords tore through innocent lives? Were you there when the Great Flood swallowed entire villages?"

"When we fought to end the vile trade of men and women stolen by pirates, were you as outraged then as you are today? Did you speak up? Did you lend a hand?"

"What about the five hundred miner dwarves—rescued not far from the very place you performed your heroic actions in the Box Canyon battle? Brilliant move, by the way. But did you care to share your thoughts on the tireless work of the Drukyl dragons—the keepers of the only reliable documents we have?"

"I don't recall seeing you advise Prince Yeled when he was deceived, abandoned and nearly lost everything before this very judge took him in. In fact, I don't recall your counsel at all."

"Are you privy to the guidance I receive from Noomai, from Nomos, from my most trusted advisors? Do you know the beginning and the end of all quests?"

"And tell me—what wisdom do you offer now, as that self-righteous fool sits before me, pretending to pass judgment in this charade of a court?"

Dolos turned to Ilyahoo, exasperated. "Prosecutor, do you wish to object?"

Ilyahoo considered it for a brief moment, then shook his head. "Hmm... nope, Your Honor. I don't think I do. Thanks for asking, though. No objection."

The King's gaze returned to Reggie—softer now, yet no less commanding. "My son, my knight... have you spoken with my other knights? Each of them knighted after enduring quests they found impossible. Each of them failed miserably. And yet today, they serve me with unwavering loyalty. They would go anywhere, fight any battle, sacrifice everything for the people they swore to protect—including you."

Reggie clenched his jaw. He turned abruptly to Ilya at the prosecution table, his voice low but urgent.

"Is there anything we can do to stop this?"

"In what sense do you mean stop?" Ilya asked, keeping an eye on the judge.

"I mean... stop the proceedings."

"No. Once a trial has begun, unless the judge deems it so,

it cannot be stopped. In the end, this banana court must determine if the King is or is not guilty of unfaithfulness."

"So there is nothing I can do? Can I get a moment to think?"

"Your honor," said Ilya, addressing the judge. "My client needs a moment. I request a recess."

This served the judge well. He'd been looking for an excuse to end the King's strange rant. He wasn't sure what the King was thinking, but it couldn't be good. In all of it, the King had walked the tightrope, making sure he didn't break the deal. He never told Reggie why he hadn't intervened. If he had, the deal would have been forfeit, and he would have lost the wager. But he had abided strictly by the rules of the game.

"Very well," said Dolos. "I think we could all use a break from the foolishness of the last witness. The King is dismissed to go back to his castle and do whatever silliness he does."

"I believe I might stick around," said the King knowingly, with a smirk. His plan was coming together. He would stick around to watch the fireworks. "I love a good drama, particularly when it involves roasted gorgon," quipped the King, as he rose and found a seat alongside Nomos. Nomos was about to burst into laughter. For the first time, the court's lead strategist was beginning to see the bigger picture of this whole thing.

"We will reconvene in 15 minutes," said an increasingly frustrated Dolos—banging his gavel—looking pale and worried.

14

THE SECOND WITNESS

The prosecutor brought Reggie back to a nearby vacant conference room. "Ilya, give me a moment, please. I need to speak to Felix alone."

"Very well. I think I may have an idea, but I need to check the legal archives. I'll be back in 10 minutes."

After he left, Reggie took a deep breath and addressed his only friend in the world—the only one he completely trusted right now.

"Hey, buddy. I need you to do something important. Will you do that for me?"

"Hey, sure. What's up?" asked Felix.

"Do you still have the CBT 5000?"

"Yep, right here." He handed it to Reggie.

"I want you to look at me through it and tell me everything it says."

"Wow, that's awkward, dude. Are you sure?"

"Yeah. If you think it's awkward, imagine how I feel. But it's important. I'm having trouble figuring out what's going on

in my head. I'm so confused. I'm not even sure why I'm here
—or who I am anymore. It's all so very strange."

"Wow. We man-bags have another saying: 'Yesterday's
weirdness is tomorrow's reason why.' We hope. What are you
expecting it to say?"

"That's just it. A few days ago, I was sure of who I was
and what I felt. But all these levels... they've exposed
something deeper within me—something in my heart. Now, I
am not sure of anything. I can't explain it. I just need some
truth."

"Doctor, prepare the patient for surgery," Felix quipped,
trying to lighten the mood. "You will be sorry when you get
my bill—my services aren't covered by your health care
plan."

"Let's get this over with," Reggie said, steady now..

For the next 10 minutes, Felix described everything he
saw in Reggie's reflection through the CBT 5000.

At times, Reggie couldn't hold back the tears. That was
new for him. He had never been one to cry much. In the
past, he fought such human emotions, fearing it showed
weakness and vulnerability—or so he told himself. But now
he realized it was a normal, common defense mechanism
designed to shield himself from being hurt again. Nothing
cut deeper than broken relationships—and Reggie had seen
more than his share. So his brain built walls. If he showed no
sign of vulnerability and never got too close to anyone, he
wouldn't suffer hurt again. But then, this. He'd been wrong.
It turned out that those same walls also blocked out the good
stuff.

Felix answered every one of Reggie's questions as best he
could. Reggie realized how wrong he'd been about so many
things. Now, he wondered how he could become the Reggie

he was always meant to be. It was time for him to take the stand. He wasn't looking forward to it.

There was a knock on the conference room door.

"Reggie, we need to talk. I found a very obscure legal loophole. I've never used it, and I've never seen it used—but perhaps it could work."

"Okay, now we're getting somewhere."

"As your counsel, I must inform you that there may be consequences."

"Like what?" Reggie asked, worried.

"Well, for one, you will be giving up your desire to get any immediate answers from the King."

"Okay, let's say that's the case. What can I do?"

"You can formerly request that the court officially 'delay the resolution of your case.' Those are the exact legal words you must use. The charges will still be on the books. Think of it as tabling the case until later. 'Later' is to be determined by some undisclosed means in the future. The case and charges are still pending—just delayed. So, the King will not be found guilty of anything, at least not yet."

"How long can such a trial be delayed?"

"Indefinitely, I suppose. We will need the support of defense counsel, but I imagine Noomai will quickly see what we are trying to do."

"Okay, I'm in. What do I need to do?"

"I will need to put you on the stand. Are you good with that?"

"What are we waiting for?" Reggie responded, a glimmer of hope shining in his eyes, the first he had felt in many days.

"Prosecutor, are you prepared to continue without any more delay?" asked Dolos.

"Yes, Judge, I would like to call Reggie Blackstone to the stand."

Dolos' brows knit together with concern. Something told him the boy was going to do something rash. He was like a nasty fly that keeps buzzing around your face—you can't get rid of it. And Dolos knew something about flies. Reggie was like the next Marvel sequel that just keeps coming, with no end in sight. But there was little Dolos could do about it.

"Defense," said Dolos to Noomai, "Any objection to the plaintiff taking the stand?"

Noomai looked over at Ilyahoo just in time to see him wink.

"No," she said hesitantly. "No objection at this time."

"Very well, counselor. Call your witness."

"Reggie, take a deep breath. You've been through a lot in the past two days, but you are safe here. No harm can come to you. I need you to speak freely," the prosecutor instructed.

"Yes, of course," Reggie replied, still worried if he could share what he had learned.

"You brought these charges against the King for two reasons. First, you seek vindication. You feel you were being punished for something you don't remember doing. Is that right?"

"Yes."

"Second, you fear you have fallen from the King's favor. Does that sound accurate?"

Reggie nodded. "Yes."

"Is there anything else you'd like to share with the court?"

Reggie took a deep breath. "Please bear with me. I think this is very relevant."

He paused.

"During the recess, I spent time reflecting—using the Mirror of Truth, CBT 5000. I was shocked at how little I genuinely understand about myself—why I act the way I do, why I hold back, why I keep friends at a distance. Honestly, I'm not even aware I do that."

"Word!" inserted Felix. Many in the audience chuckled.

"The truth is," Reggie continued, "I've been emotionally crippled, and I didn't even realize it. I carry some wounds, I guess—deep scars from broken relationships that never healed."

The courtroom was silent, hanging on his every word.

"The defense counsel is aware that I don't have parents anymore. They were assassinated by anti-King loyalists in Qayeen when I was eight. I guess I've been on my own ever since. The Drukyl dragons have been quite kind to me—if I have a family, it's them." He hesitated before adding, "And of course, Felix."

Felix cleared his throat, shifting in place, "Double Word."

Reggie managed a weak smile. "Felix, my best friend—the magic man-bag. But other than that, I keep my emotional distance. I always have. I didn't choose it; my brain built walls to keep me from being hurt again."

Tears welled in Noomai's compassionate eyes.

"One thing the Mirror of Truth revealed to me—I wasn't

planning to share this, but I think I must—is that deep in some dark corner of my mind, I still blame myself for my parents' deaths."

A hushed murmur rippled through the courtroom.

"Logically, I know I was an eight-year-old kid. I couldn't have done anything. But there's still this cruel dragon voice in my head whispering that it was my fault, that I failed them."

He exhaled shakily. "And then, months ago, something strange happened. During the knighting ceremony, when I looked into the King's eyes... I saw my mother's eyes. I felt her warmth. And for the first time in years, something inside me opened—a little, anyway. I wasn't alone anymore. I had a father again—a real family. Or so I thought."

Reggie paused, composing himself as the weight of his own words settled over the room. By now, tears were flowing down the Great King's cheeks.

"Do you need some water, Reggie?" asked Ilya.

"No, I'm good. Let me get through this before I fall apart." Reggie took a deep breath. "But then... everything shattered." His voice tightened. "I was illegally kidnapped— thrown into a game I never agreed to play, forced to survive impossible trials, each one deadlier than the last. I barely made it through. And all the while, I kept waiting—waiting for the King to come for me. That's what good fathers do, right? Help. Acknowledge me. Have my back."

He clenched his fists.

"But he never did."

The audience gasped. The King shut his eyes. A large, weepy dwarf in the audience blew his nose loudly. A few people shushed him.

"I felt like I'd lost another father. Deep down, I believed it was my fault—again." His voice cracked. "That's why I'm angry. Angry at the King—for not having my back. Angry at myself—for whatever I did to make him turn away."

The weepy dwarf blew his nose even louder this time. More shushing.

"I needed to know what I did wrong. What didn't I do? What words did I say—or fail to say? Was this family so fragile that I lost it in just a few days? Or worse… is there something about me that makes me unworthy of a father's love? Maybe no father would ever truly have me—not when it mattered."

A heavy silence swept over the courtroom.

"Did your captors make it worse?" asked the prosecutor.

"Oh yes, absolutely," Reggie continued, his voice lower now. "They told me the King knew where I was. That he had allowed it—it was his idea. He had turned his back on me. He never cared."

"And did you believe them?" the prosecutor inquired gently.

"Not at first. No. But the longer I went without hearing from him… the harder it was to ignore."

The prosecutor nodded empathetically. "Before you took the stand today, you said you had a request for the court."

"Yes." Reggie straightened.

"Please, go on," said Ilya.

"I formally request that this case be delayed. I believe those are the right words. I want to table my trial until a later date, to be determined."

"Objection!" Judge Dolos cried out in rage. He had been caught totally unaware—and he hated surprises.

"Your Honor, with all due respect, you can't object," the prosecutor countered. "There is legal precedent. I direct your attention to *Wade v. Raxbut*—the case regarding the theft of

500 dragon saddles. Raxbut claimed he had already sold them, but Wade, unwilling to risk public scrutiny over his false charges, requested that the case be tabled indefinitely. Though outright dismissal was not allowed once the trial had begun, the court permitted a delay to an undetermined future date, with the defense's agreement."

"We request the same outcome today," said Reggie's attorney.

Dolos' face darkened. The audience couldn't believe what had happened, and some stood and cheered. Dolos slammed his gavel repeatedly. "Order! Order! Order in my court!" He took a sharp, frustrated breath, then barked, "Attorneys, approach the bench. Now!"

Noomai was grinning from ear to ear as she approached, leaning carefully on her cane. Ilya was trying very hard to keep a straight face.

"What is going on here?" Dolos hissed in a whisper, his sharp eyes flicking between them. "Yahoo—or whatever your name is—do you call this representing your client? The boy needs closure. There must be justice."

Ilyahoo remained composed. "Yes, Your Honor. My client agrees with you—there must be vindication. There must be justice." His gaze locked onto the judge's. "But he wants to delay that necessary justice until an appropriate future time. As I stated, there is an airtight legal precedent. This is his right under the kingdom's law."

Dolos exhaled through his nose. "For that to stand," he added, now grasping for a legal foothold, "uh... the defense must agree to the delay. Counselor for the defendant, surely you want the King's name cleared immediately, am I right?"

"Oh no, we truly agree with the prosecution, Your Honor," Noomai said smoothly. Then, with a knowing glint in her eye, she added, "But I'd like to ask Reggie directly on cross-examination, if I may. That is the prosecution's right."

Dolos didn't understand exactly what was happening, but he sensed the entire thing unraveling right under his nose. He tried to figure out what the King was up to, but he couldn't see it.

Noomai, feeling a little feisty and a lot impatient, took a deliberate step closer and lowered her voice for Dolos. "And Judge... don't make me come back to your bench again. You remember what I can do?"

A flicker of terror flashed in Dolos' gaze. She was not to be taken lightly. He stiffened, then rudely waved them back to their respective tables.

Clearing his throat, he announced, "Defense, you may proceed with your cross-examination."

Noomai turned to Reggie, her voice warm yet firm.

"Reggie, thank you for your testimony. You've been through so much. We all understand your feelings—your longing for family, your fear of losing them, blaming yourself for your losses. That isn't brokenness. That's *human*."

Reggie swallowed hard.

"You, dear boy, have suffered great loss and betrayal. No one here blames you for taking the King to trial."

That wasn't what he was expecting to hear.

She took a slight step forward. "Now, let me clarify what you truly desire. Do you want to table this case against the King—to delay it until a yet-to-be-determined time?"

Reggie took a breath. "Yes, ma'am. I do."

Noomai studied him carefully. "What about vindication?

Your feelings of abandonment? The accusation that the King failed you. What about the answers you still don't have?"

Reggie's fists tightened on the stand. "Of course, I still want those things. I do." He hesitated, then exhaled. "And if that's wrong, then I'm wrong. If that means the King will never speak to me again... I get it. Maybe I deserve that."

Silence. Even the air in the courtroom seemed still.

"All I'm saying," Reggie continued, his voice steadier, "is that I'm willing to admit how little I understand. There's a mountain of things I don't know—things I may never grasp. And perhaps, buried in that pile... there's a reason for my suffering."

His voice softened, and he looked to the floor. "I hope so, anyway."

His eyes swept the room. "I see now that there is so much about the King and his ways that I can't fathom. I see this world through a narrow keyhole... but the King sees the whole battlefield."

His throat tightened.

"For the life of me, I can't imagine why he wouldn't speak to me. But I'm willing to believe—just believe—and hope—that there might be a reason I cannot yet comprehend."

A deep breath. A quiet strength settled into his bones.

"So, yes—I regret initiating this trial. I regret disrupting all your lives. I regret I may have... likely have... offended many of you. I know I have let you down. I know this has changed how you see me."

His hands unclenched.

"I accept that."

A pause. A beat of stillness before the final words left his lips.

"I can live with all that. But the thing I regret most," Reggie met the eyes of all those in the courtroom.

"I regret if I have done anything to tarnish the name of the King."

A murmur of approval rippled through the court.

"Triple word!" Felix exclaimed.

"I'm willing to accept that he had his reasons. Reasons far above my understanding." He looked down at his hands.

"And I hope—someday—I'll get my answers."

His gaze lifted, calm but resolute.

"But I choose not to need them today."

"Pssst," said Felix from Reggie's side. "Hey buddy, can we talk?"

"Excuse me, counselor. Can I have a moment to talk to my man-bag?"

"Please, go ahead," agreed Noomai with a tender smile.

Reggie and Felix whispered back and forth for some time. At one point, Reggie laughed out loud, "Really? You are too much, dude."

"Okay, I am ready again. Uh, I am not quite sure how to proceed, but in addition to tabling the trial against the King, I would like to make a formal charge against the judge of the court."

As Reggie's final words echoed through the courtroom, the justice chamber erupted with cheers. Judge Dolos' fingers twitched against the dais, his knuckles whitening around the gavel. His lips curled, revealing an unsettling grin—one that stretched too wide, too unnatural.

In an instant, the transformation began. A sickening crack sounded as Dolos' spine arched backward, his elegant judicial robes shredding into tattered, serpentine rags. His skin, once pale and stately, hardened into ashen-gray scales. His refined features twisted and contorted—his nose flattening, his mouth stretching into a grotesque maw lined with needle-like fangs. His dignified powdered wig sloughed off, revealing a nest of writhing, venomous serpents that screeched and hissed in unison.

His bulbous, yellow eyes bulged, straining in their sockets —more animal than anything else, totally devoid of mercy, bereft of reason.

A guttural, unearthly roar exploded from his arched throat, shaking the very foundations of the courtroom. The wooden panels splintered. The towering marble columns cracked. The stained-glass windows shattered, raining jagged shards upon the stunned audience.

Panic erupted. Most in the audience bolted for the doors, their shrieks swallowed by the deafening wail of Dolos' transformation. The once-orderly courtroom descended into chaos—benches overturned, parchment scattered like autumn leaves in a storm.

Dolos rose above them, his form no longer human but something ancient, something cursed. His voice, layered with a thousand hissing, serpentine whispers, boomed through the chamber:

"STREET RAT, YOU THINK YOU CAN ESCAPE JUSTICE? YOU THINK YOU CAN DEFY ME? THIS TRIAL IS FAR FROM OVER!" The gorgon spat, full of deep rage. "THIS IS MY COURT. YOU HAVE NO JURISDICTION HERE!"

Reggie, heart pounding, knew now with some clarity that this wasn't just a trial anymore. It never was. This was war.

"Ah, but your honor, *I* do," said Ilyahoo, the prosecutor, calmly and without fear of the gorgon.

"Bailiff, please arrest the judge on the charges of

kidnapping, abuse, attempted murder, bad hygiene and overall rudeness."

"Mr. Prosecutor, may I offer a suggestion that could save the justice system both time and expense?" Noomai asked calmly—strikingly calm compared to Dolos.

"Of course," said Ilya, knowingly.

"Pure dead brilliant!" blurted out Nomos with an impish grin. "What took ye so long?"

"What, and miss all the fun of watching Dolos show his true colors?" retorted Noomai.

Noomai looked over at Reggie, who was still in the witness chair. "Reggie, would you be a dear and join me? I am not sure that I have the strength to do this on my own anymore. I am confident you are the right one to help this time. What do you say?"

Reggie couldn't believe it. "You want me—after all the mess I've caused, everything I've done and said—to do the rolling-up-the-world thingy?"

"Of course, dear boy. Haven't you heard? There is nothing you could ever do to lose the favor of this King—or me."

"Or me, Laddie," said Nomos as he stood to assist the two with Dolos—if need be. "Lang may yer lum reek (may you live long and prosper)."

Up until now, the King had barely moved. He sat filled with a great sense of satisfaction, certain all was about to end as he imagined. He smiled a royal smile. But now it was time to play his royal role. He rose and moved toward Reggie, arms open wide. As he hugged him with a fatherly hug, he said for all to hear:

"Reggie, you are my son—my honorable, heroic son—with whom I am well pleased. Nothing can or will ever change that. I know that at times, you will doubt the veracity of that statement. Still, I promise you, I will always have your back... not always the way you envision, Sir Reggie," he bowed graciously. "This next assignment is for you alone. Counselor, proceed. I can't take any more of the stench in this courtroom."

"So, Sir Reggie Brownstone, faithful son of the Great King of Garden City," said Noomai graciously, "stand here and raise your hands toward the upper corners of the room. Good. Now repeat after me: Enough foul imp. You have no authority here. We are of the King."

Dolos couldn't believe it. It was all planned perfectly. All contingencies had been imagined. Yet he had been defeated once again. He found himself helpless in the hands of another —this time not Nomos, or the King, or even Noomai, but a gangly teenage boy—and his rude pouch, of course.

Felix couldn't stop snickering.

"You abominable deceiver," Noomai continued. "Isn't it enough that you are allowed for a time to roam around the valleys and do your destruction? And yet you still seek to challenge the King and undermine his will—and now his justice. Will you never learn your place? Your arrogance is beyond measure. You have no authority here."

Reggie repeated everything just as Noomai said.

"Okay," said Noomai. "Now flick your hand in his face— like you're swatting a nasty bug."

"If it is okay, Noomai," said Reggie with a smile, "I've got this from here. I have seen it done once before. Is it okay if Felix has a shot?"

"Of course, he has earned it."

"Gorgonzola," quipped Felix, enjoying himself tremendously, "in the end, you will wear out like a garment, like a thin, flimsy robe; you will be rolled up and tossed like the rest of the trash into the fire and burned."

Reggie smiled, rose up on his tiptoes, grabbed the very corners of the courtroom and rolled it up like it was a beat-up old stage backdrop—then kicked it aside. No more Dolos, no more dais, no more courtroom at all.

Everyone was now standing in the Great King's throne room, rejoicing that, once more, Dolos had been defeated.

15

FINALE?

"Three cheers for Sir Reginald Blackstone and Sir Felix, the greatest and most faithful of all the knights who serve me and my kingdom."

The Great King of Garden City stood before his throne behind the grand table of honor, speaking to the many friends, family and supporters that filled the royal ballroom. They had come—men, women, elves, halflings, dragons, dwarves, trolls and many others from Garden City and Amaratzim—to honor Reggie and Felix's defeat of the vile gorgon, Dolos. Sir Reggie and Sir Felix had crushed the head of the gorgon twice now. Songs and stories of their most recent, dangerous quest would be sung for generations.

All joined in. "Three cheers for Reggie and Felix. Huzzah! Huzzah! Huzzah!"

The audience agreed in unison. "Three cheers for Reggie and Felix. Huzzah! Huzzah! Huzzah!"

Reggie had taken his seat between Nomos and me, Jeremy, at the head table. He placed Felix on the table in front of him. This celebration was for the man-bag, too.

The honorable Eiren Opoios, the President Prime Minister of Qayeen, was on the other side of Nomos. But despite all the dignitaries who gathered to celebrate the completion of this unique quest, Reggie was still not fully able to enjoy the victory celebration. Not yet anyway. His head was still swimming over the whole quest ordeal.

"Ya see, laddie," said an exuberant Nomos just moments before, "the King knew better than all of us what was goin' on. I'll admit, I was teeterin' on doubtin' him m'self till the very end. But I'm reminded again—he's a master o' quests, usin' 'em freely as a way tae share his glory wi' the rest o' us."

"I still can't wrap my head around it all," said the boy. "At its core, this was a quest? Ordained by the King himself? That changes everything I ever thought about quests."

"I second that," quipped Felix. "You know, we man-bags have an ancient saying. 'If it looks like a duck and quacks like a duck, well, it isn't a fire-breathing Cambrian Swamp Escridemion'—if you know what I mean."

"Well, here's the wee secret, lad," said Nomos, ignoring Felix's... uh... interesting contribution to the conversation. "Ye weren't picked for the quest because you did something wrong, but because ye didn't. That slimy worm figured that if he could turn ye away from the King, he could turn anyone. It was diabolical, I'll grant ye. But the King knew ye were the most faithful around. He trusted ye."

It was so strange. One moment, Reggie and Felix were in a courtroom, sending Dolos to who knows where. The next moment, they were at the head table in the King's massive ballroom, filled with well-wishers and autograph hounds.

"Huzzah, huzzah for the gorgon head crusher, Sir Reggie Blackstone!" cried one warrior in full knight garb, his chest covered in medals marking him as a true hero in the service of the King.

"Huzzah, huzzah, huzzah!" the crowd roared its approval again.

The ghostly specter of Berenice, the legendary storyteller herself, hovered toward the head table and wrapped her spirit arms around our hero—well, through him. Such spirits can't be heard, but she mouthed the words: "I am so proud of you. I would never have been able to do such a quest. The King was right to choose you." Then she fluttered off—if that's the right way to describe it. Reggie was blown away, of course.

Then he turned to Nomos and asked the obvious question, "But why couldn't I be let in on the joke?"

"Ach, can ye no' see? That was part o' the King's trap! It made the end so much worse for the serpent!"

"But why couldn't you or anyone else tell me what was going on?"

"Same reason, lad. Then it wouldn't be a fair wager. Anyone can survive if they know that there's a higher purpose. Ye had to rely on your deep internal belief in the King, even when that nasty, critical inner dragon voice in your skull did not see eye to eye with ya."

"By the time o' the trial, that blasted dust-eater was so overconfident he never expected ye tae do anythin'—but ye did! For all time, he'll bear the scars ye gave him on this quest. Oh, he'll remember ye, that's for sure. An' so will we! Generations from now, folk will tell the tale o' yer strange quest. I suppose Dolos will need another humiliatin' lesson someday, but he won't be choosin' you again... will he?"

"Nomos, it is still quite troubling to me. How can the King send someone like me on such a quest without permission? That doesn't seem right or fair."

"Aye, I said the same thing tae Noomai when we heard the wager. Ye know what she told me? She asked when I last saw a fair or right quest. That's no' the kind the King imagines. Almost every quest ends in abysmal failure... till somethin' happens. Noomai calls it a *eucatastrophe*—when everythin' flips on its head an' the gorgon takes another nosedive intae the privy."

"She believed—even though arrogant Dolos seemed tae set the whole thing up—it was all the King's doin' in the end. I see it now. He masterfully manipulated that ijit shadow lord like a fisherman lures a daft fish tae bite. Dolos thought ye— with all yer emotional baggage—would be the perfect pawn tae undermine the King. But the King saw it differently. He saw ye as the only one who could truly defeat Dolos at his own game an' drag him through his own filth. Ye were the one to crush the head of the serpent."

"This was never about testin' yer faithfulness or loyalty, lad. No... this was an honor given tae ye *because* of yer already steadfast faith. It was a gift, from a proud father tae his loyal son. Aye, that's what he is. Don't ever doubt it again. He foreknew that ye'd best Dolos—an' soundly—even wi' one hand tied behind yer back. Or both!"

"Think about it. If the King had asked yer permission an' told ye what was ahead—would ye have done it?"

"No... of course not," said Reggie.

"Exactly, lad! Ye're loyal, not daft. There's nae real quest o' value—at least, none designed by this King—that doesnae feel unfair in the middle. The quester will almost always feel like a failure, feel isolated an' unworthy. But that's the point, isn't it?"

"Quests arenae designed in this kingdom tae earn the King's favor—the questers already have it! They arenae designed to test faithfulness and loyalty. No—the quests are meant tae make the quester feel that favor all the more. I've told many a knight the same thing. The fiercest an' most terrifyin' dragons in a quest don't live in caves or fly the skies spewin' fire. No, lad, they're the ones whisperin' inside yer skull, tellin' ye that ye're unworthy o' the King's love. The greatest quests are the ones that silence those filthy, lyin' dragons once an' for all."

"An' this quest... it made ye see somethin' about yerself an' the King, did it no'?"

"Aye... and at least for that, I am eternally grateful," agreed Reggie.

"So, it was truly a twofer, ye see then! The gorgon was defeated by the very weapon he designed tae use against the King. An' secondly, the quester has learned a great truth about the nature o' this King's love. For those two reasons alone—though I reckon there's more at play—ye were chosen for this quest long before Dolos started schemin'. The King is no' what he appears, that much is certain."

"But I failed the King! That troubles me the most. I took the King to court," said Reggie, with furrowed eyes.

"Aye, that? Ach, lad, that was nothin'! 'Course ye did! Ye're no' an unfeelin', narcissistic psychopath. There's only one o' those in the kingdom—well, maybe two."

"Ah, but somethin' inside ye bubbled up—as the King knew it would—an' ye ended up doin' the right thing. Ye crushed the gorgon's entire plan. Flushed it straight down the sewer, ye did! I'm so proud o' ye, laddie."

"I think I can help here," said Rahgornah, the Drukyl dragon who had lumbered up to the opposite side of the head table from the others. He was far too big to sit at the table. He was used to that. He was relegated to standing, and even then, he had to duck to avoid hitting the high chandeliers. Rahgornah, the Drukyl dragon, stood more than 50 feet tall with a massive wingspan. His deep indigo and stormy gray scales shimmered like polished gems—each edged with electric blue. Jagged, lightning-like horns crowned his head, and his molten gold eyes gleamed with sharp intelligence. Oddly, he wore thick-lensed spectacles, giving him the air of a colossal, reptilian scholar. When he spoke, his voice rumbled like distant thunder—controlled, yet powerful enough to bring down the rafters if unleashed.

[Storyteller's Note: Rahgornah the Black, a wise and ancient Sakalon dragon, resides in the Drukyl Mountains of northern Amaratzim. Tasked by the Great King, the Sakalon serve as faithful guardians of the Royal Reliable Documents (RRD)— the complete, approved record of the Kingdom's Tales. These tales hold the true history of all so-be'd quests, past and future, revealing not just what happened, but why. Isn't it reassuring to know that a sacred document, protected by mighty dragons, holds the answers to all your quest's "why" questions?]

"The Reliable Document," said Rahgornah, "is full of poems, cries and dirges of faithful servants of the King who, like you, couldn't balance the scales. They couldn't reconcile what they knew about the King and how they were being treated. Some are downright condemning. But, like you, in the end, they proclaimed that they would still trust the King despite what they saw. I am reminded of one very poignant poem."

"O Great King of Garden City,
I cry out day and night before you.
Turn your ear to my cry!
For my soul is full of troubles,
and my life draws near to the grave.
It is you who have put me in the depths of the pit,
it is your wrath that lies heavy upon me,
and you overwhelm me with all your waves."

"My brave brother, I imagine you know exactly what the poet was saying, don't you?"

"So, did the King punish that doubting poet?" Reggie asked, tilting his head slightly.

"Oh no. Our King's shoulders are broad and can handle a great deal of criticism and doubt. He said it in his trial. He has been called much worse. Let's face it, his ways are so much higher than our ways. Sometimes, they are troubling. That poem is proudly included in a place of great honor in the Reliable Documents."

"With a silent *h*," quipped Felix.

The Royal Counselor, Noomai, walked very carefully over to Reggie's table. "Reggie, you did so well. I wasn't sure at first what you were going to say in court. I am very impressed. I can see what the King sees in you. Did you know there is a very wise scribe who openly asked the question, 'Why do bad things happen to good people?'

Reggie, isn't that the same question you were wrestling with?"

"Yes, I suppose it is. What was his answer?"

"Honestly, his quest was to ask the question that so many others dare not ask. But I think you may have the real answer."

"Maybe. I don't think my current answer is going to help anyone, but here it goes: Bad things happen to good people for evil reasons, of course. However, there is also a vast, yet strange, category of bad things happening to good people for good reasons, too—perhaps even a peculiar path to a reward. Does that make any sense at all?"

Noomai hugged Reggie for a very long time.

That's when I chimed in with so many questions. "Okay, Reggie, I am responsible for telling the tale of *Shadowbound*. I don't know where to begin. Maybe we need to unpack your last statement."

"Let me take a shot," said Felix, channeling his inner erudite professor. "Dolos will regularly use good and evil only for evil purposes, while the King will use good and evil only for good purposes."

"Yikes, now that's a bumper sticker," I said. "Can I quote you, Felix?"

"Well said, my favorite magic man-bag," said Noomai with a chuckle. "That is very sophisticated and far-reaching. But we must also remember compassion. Many people are experiencing such great evil with such great losses. For them, the pain of being called to such quests is so blinding that they will not be able to gain much comfort from hearing that the King is working a higher good, partly through their losses. Such awareness will take time—a lot of time in some cases."

"My brave Reggie, what say you? Are you beginning to

experience some comfort knowing the King had never abandoned you? That he was working each of the Shadowbound quest trials for your ultimate good?"

There was a long silence as Reggie pondered the question. He was beginning to feel very fatigued. He had been through so much, and of course, he was trying to come to grips with the swirling emotions twisting wildly in his head.

"So, in *The Garden Tale*," I said, breaking the awkward silence and taking Reggie off the hook for now, "Anelé and I were attacked and almost killed by a deranged mob who had been worked up by misinformation sent by Dolos. Counselor, you're saying that the King was behind that?"

Noomai responded, choosing her words with care. "In one sense, yes, of course. In another, no. It is indeed a great, unresolvable paradox. Those people would tell you that they were acting according to their own desires and choice—and of course they were. And yet, behind the scenes, something bigger and higher was also taking place, working in conjunction with that—not against it. Our minds tend to oversimplify such things, often making them seem like either-or decisions. It is either entirely free will or a celestial puppet master who completely ignores people's agency. But what is the possibility that both exist together, equally, overlapping and yet separate?"

"Ah, yes, a classic dialectic," pontificated the professorial Felix, shocking everyone at the table. "Opposing thesis and antithesis working toward a synthesis greater than either—that was hardly obvious in the beginning."

Those around the table stopped everything in wonder at Felix's thoughts.

"What? I told you I read very widely," huffed the man-bag.

"Wait, how do you read without…" I asked.

"Don't go there, Jeremy," Reggie said, cutting me off. "You'll only get him going on a rabbit trail."

Noomai picked up where she left off. "Your quest, brave Jeremy, at that point seemed lost. But nothing was further from the truth, and yet you still had an important part to play —decisions to make and the courage to make them. The King's so-be'd quests work in full cahoots with our choices, doubts and will. Some philosophers from other kingdoms wax eloquent about fate and fortune acting as controlling plot lines. We know better and understand far less."

Now Nomos blundered in with a huge rap on Reggie's shoulders. "Boy, I am so proud of ye. Yer quest was tae singlehandedly—well, wi' the help o' the Drukyls and Felix—crush the gorgon's skull for the second time in a few weeks. Ye now share in the King's glory as one o' the greatest gorgon crushers ever! Few have had that honor: Noomai an' Anele—and now ye. What an honor, eh? Though I ken well, ye never asked for it, did ye?"

"No…" Reggie responded, still overwhelmed with all the new information.

"Ach, no matter! Yer one of the few in the kingdom's history who's defeated that beast while bein' completely in the dark about the true nature an' end o' yer quest. All of it was designed tae maximize the shame o' that nasty lizard—his embarrassment, his loss o' honor. And ye did it! The King chose ye, out o' all folk, tae be his agent o' defeat against the squid—because ye were the most worthy."

"Three cheers for my son, Sir Reggie, one of the greatest knights in my kingdom," cried the Great King.

"Huzzah! Huzzah! Huzzah!"

Back to the King and his thoughts.

"Many of you here tonight are troubled by the shocking nature of the quest that Reggie and Felix were launched into only a few days ago," the King began, his voice grave and clear. "I would be cold and indifferent to suggest you should not be troubled. In fact, I would say this: It is only right to be concerned. It is natural—expected, even—to wrestle with the reality—no, the probability—of such difficult-to-swallow quests in my kingdom."

He paused, then continued more quietly. "My young and faithful knight was thrown into a violent, dangerous journey. He had no warning. He did not seek it, and he certainly did not agree to it. And due to its very nature, he was virtually alone. I could not speak to him. I could not shield him. That was not negligence—that was the design of the quest itself."

Another pregnant pause. This one heavier. "And I was the designer."

A collective gasp rippled through the assembly. For many, this was the first time they'd heard it; that the Great King—not Dolos—had been the ultimate architect of Reggie's harrowing ordeal.

"But hear me clearly. It was never my intention to use such a quest to test this young man's loyalty or to measure his faithfulness to me. I already knew the strength of his devotion. It was precisely that extraordinary loyalty that made him one of the few I would entrust with a task of such magnitude. I knew he would be victorious—not because I gambled on his success, but because I knew his worth."

He looked across the room. The silence deepened.

"He wasn't cast into Dolos' slimy grasp to prove himself to me. He was sent *because* of who he already was."

"And what was the task?" the King asked rhetorically. "To stand firm on his inner faithfulness and battle one of the most wicked deceivers to ever prowl the lands of my kingdom. Dolos—the manipulator, the slanderer, the gaslighter of old—whose eternal aim is to undermine my throne and smear my name. That oily squidface has always believed that no human could remain loyal unless I constantly bribed or babied them. In his shriveled mind, loyalty must be purchased."

"But," the King's voice swelled, "my sons, Reggie and Felix, you proved him wrong. You did what few could. You crushed the deceiver's skull—and with it, you shattered his cynical view of humanity. And yes," he added with a wry smile, "of man-bags, too."

Laughter broke out.

Then, his tone turned tender again.

"Sir Reggie. Sir Felix. I have *never* turned my back on you, though I know it felt that way. I have *never* doubted your loyalty or questioned your knighthood—though, in the depths of Shadowbound, it surely seemed like I had. And listen carefully: I have never been more—or less—pleased with either of you before or after the quest. My favor toward you was never conditional on your success. Not then, not now."

He stepped forward.

"And as people across the kingdom hear your story, the true nature of my favor will shine clearer than ever. That is your gift to them."

He drew in a breath.

"This quest you endured ranks among the top five most grueling quests of all time. Only my most courageous and faithful knights would have survived it. Fewer still would have conquered the gorgon. And of those, even fewer would have emerged faithful—still honoring my name and throne."

"You did both."

"Huzzah! Huzzah! Huzzah!"

The King stepped forward and wrapped his royal arms around the silent lad and his pouch. He hugged them both tightly—for a long time. And before all, royal tears flowed freely down the King's cheeks.

Later, Reggie shared something with me. Two things, actually —both began in that moment. He has given me permission to share them with you now.

First, as he looked into the tearful eyes of the King of Garden City... he became convinced—again—that he saw his mother's eyes.

Second, something even more mysterious. He began to feel the favor of the King—the very favor he had come to doubt throughout the bitter trials of Shadowbound. The pain wasn't gone. The questions hadn't vanished. But somehow, mysteriously, he would now begin to process them with the King at his side, the King's smile shining over him.

And for true knights of the realm... *that* makes all the difference.

16

ONE MONTH LATER

He's back in Buzah, you know," said the elderly man, leaning on a stick, his white hair wilder than a hedgewolf in heat. "Actually. Both of them."

"Are they the right ones? You know they have been through a great deal recently?" asked his companion, a beautiful fey.

"Ah. So many questions. In an ideal world, we might have other options, but what can we really do?" asked the old man, shaking his wizened head and pointing an antique broken compass in front of him as if it held the answers to all his questions.

"My compass is pointing that direction—without a doubt. I must trust it."

A pause.

"Here's another question," she added. "Why would he help us? This isn't really his problem."

"No," said the old man, sad eyes glinting, "but it soon will be. That much is certain. If it can happen in our world, why would Garden City escape such a fate?"

"What am I missing here? He's not a qualified mapmaker. A street magician? Neither is the magic man-bag?"

"Hmph," grumbled the old man. "And, they are both warrior-knights. They helped stop an entire world war in Amaratzim, and have faced the evil gorgon Dolos twice and won. The Great King recognizes something in him and his companion. So do I."

"What is a man-pouch anyway?" asked the fey.

"Man-bag, actually. He's oddly sensitive about that."

"So I've heard." A chuckle. "Still, the man-bag may have a personal quest of its own. You know about his former step-mom? I understand that she may be in some trouble. He hasn't see her since—well—for a long time."

"True," nodded the man. "But she never stopped looking for him. I wonder if that is why she is messing with fire?"

"Hmm," agreed the fey resigned that they have no choice. "It might all work out—serendipity and all that. How long do we have to decide?"

The old man squinted at the sun.

"What time is it?"

"Three."

"Then we have under six hours to get them started."

"That's far too fast."

"The timeline isn't mine. You know that as well as anyone. And our world's already unraveling. You have seen it yourself. Entire communities—forgotten, overwritten. If you replace every plank on a ship—the mast, the rigging, the sails —is it still the same ship? Is it even a ship? And then what? Will our home be a home much longer?"

"Fine," said the troubled fairy, her bright starlight wings now fluttering less brightly than before. "But it's still not fair for those two. They have no idea what they're getting into.

However, I'll do what we agreed upon. I'll hide the pieces where only a true mapmaker can find them. Then I vanish. Your plan?"

"All is lost unless I get the boy's signature. Then... I'll just have to figure it all out. Not a great plan, but it's what I've got."

"How will you draw him in?"

He grinned and unfurled a parchment.

WAREHOUSE SPACE
FOR IMMEDIATE RENT
PRICE IS RIGHT:
ONLY TWO COPPERS A MONTH

17½ HOLLOW WAY

ASK FOR BARRO.
NO APPOINTMENT NECESSARY.
DO NOT DELAY.

THAT MEANS RIGHT NOW.

MOVE IT!

WHAT ARE YOU WAITING FOR?

"I'll post it on the Street Shadows' warehouse. No way they resist that." He smiled. "Then—boom. We've got them... I hope."

The regal fey's smile faded further.

"I hope you're right," she said. 'But once he finds out they're in play…"

"King help them. They're our last chance."

"Yes." She turned her face toward the city skyline. "King help them all… and us too."

From a narrow balcony above the alley, half-shrouded in soot and ivy, Barro watched Reggie and Felix in silence.

He didn't blink.

He didn't breathe.

But the parchment in his hand rippled with unseen wind, and a single word scrawled itself across the bottom in black ink, curling like smoke.

SOON!

∾

Don't miss Reggie's and Felix's next exciting quest adventure: *The Mapmaker's Tale.*

THANKS SO MUCH!

Hey, if you enjoyed *Shadowbound*, we'd greatly appreciate your support with a review on Amazon.

Simply use the QR code below, then scroll down to *"Write a Customer Review"* near the bottom of the page. Have fun. Let your voice be heard. King-willing your enthusiastic and creative feedback will inspire other young readers—and adults—to pick up the book and enjoy.